Mary Anne and the Silent Witness

THE BABY-SITTERS CLUB

Mary Anne and the Silent Witness
Ann M. Martin

AN
APPLE
PAPERBACK

SCHOLASTIC INC.
New York Toronto London Auckland Sydney

The author gratefully acknowledges
Ellen Miles
for her help in
preparing this manuscript.

Cover art by Hodges Soileau

ISBN 0-590-22868-4

Copyright © 1996 by Ann M. Martin. All rights reserved. Published by Scholastic Inc. THE BABY-SITTERS CLUB, THE BABY-SITTERS CLUB logo, APPLE PAPERBACKS, and the APPLE PAPERBACKS logo are registered trademarks of Scholastic Inc.

12 11 10 9 8 7 6 5 4 3 2 1   6 7 8 9/9 0 1/0

Printed in the U.S.A.   40

First Scholastic printing, April 1996

CHAPTER 1

"Bye, Tiggy," I cooed, bending down to rub noses with the softest, sweetest, cutest little gray tiger kitten in the world. It was a Monday morning in early April, and if I was going to be on time for school I had to head downstairs for breakfast within the next ten seconds. But it's always so hard to say good-bye to Tigger. He'd already been downstairs for his own breakfast, and now he was back on my bed, curled up for his regularly scheduled early-morning nap. (To be followed by a mid-morning snack, a late-morning snooze, then lunch and a short play period, followed by a few early-afternoon z's, which would lead to mid-afternoon munchies, and so on. Cats sure do have it all figured out. Eat, sleep, play, eat, sleep, play. What a life.)

Anyway, it's hard to leave Tigger, but I managed. Being on time for school is important to me. I grabbed my backpack, checked my hair and my outfit one last time in the mirror, took a final glance at Tigger, and left my bedroom. Then I paused in the hallway before going down the stairs, certain I'd forgotten something. What was it? I had my math homework, and the short paper I'd written for English. I'd said good-bye to Tigger. My socks matched (I glanced down again just to make sure), and I'd remembered to grab my jean jacket in case it was chilly out. So what was it that didn't seem right?

I looked around, and when my eye lit upon a closed door down the hall, I realized what I was missing.

Dawn.

Dawn's my sister, or, to be technical about it, my stepsister. And behind that closed door is what used to be her bedroom. Now her bedroom is three thousand miles away — a situation I still haven't entirely adjusted to.

I guess I'd better back up and explain who I am and why I have a sister who doesn't live in my house. It's a little complicated, so stay with me.

My name's Mary Anne Spier. I'm thirteen and in the eighth grade at SMS (Stoneybrook Middle School), which is in Stoneybrook, Connecticut, the town where I've spent almost my whole life. I say almost because for a short time, when I was just a baby, I lived in Maynard, Iowa, with my grandparents. That was right after my mother died. At the time, my father was too overcome with grief to take care of me, so he sent me to stay with my mother's parents.

They loved having me. In fact, they loved me so much that they wanted to keep me with them forever. If my father hadn't fought for me, I might be attending MMS (Maynard Middle School), and saying good-bye to my pet hog Wilbur instead of to Tigger. And I certainly never would have met Dawn.

Dawn Schafer turned up in my life when she and her mom and her younger brother Jeff moved to Stoneybrook. Dawn's mom had grown up in Stoneybrook (just like my dad), but had moved to California, married, and had Dawn and Jeff. But that marriage wasn't meant to last. After the divorce, she brought her children back to Connecticut. When Dawn and I met, we became instant friends, which was a little unusual for me, since I'm normally very shy. She even joined this club I belong to, the Baby-sitters Club, or BSC (more about that later). Then, one day, when we were looking through some old yearbooks, we discovered that my dad (Richard) and her mom (Sharon) had dated each other when they were in high school, but had sadly parted ways. We thought that was the most romantic thing we'd ever heard of. We were wrong.

The most romantic thing was when we brought the two of them back together and they wound up falling in love again, and getting married!

Thinking about their wedding can bring sentimental tears to my eyes, even now. That's the way I've always been. I cry easily, and the silliest things can make me feel all choked up. My boyfriend, Logan Bruno (the cutest boy at SMS, *and* the sweetest), likes to tease me about that.

Marrying Sharon brought about some real changes in my father's personality. He'd always been fairly strict with me, I think because he was raising me on his own. (He was also trying to prove to my grandparents that he could handle the job of raising me.) He used to make me wear little-girl clothes, for example, and keep my room decorated in little-girl style. To be honest, my dad was coming around even before he met Sharon (I'd begun to convince him that I was a responsible young woman), but now he's really loosened up. Although "loose" is a relative term in my father's case. He's still the neatest, most organized person I know — next to me. (We both arrange our closets according to season and our sock drawers according to color, for example.) Sharon, by the way, is his (our) total opposite: She's a bit of a flake when it comes to sticking to schedules or keeping things tidy. (She's been known to save balancing the checkbook for a "rainy day" — which never comes — and has more than once forgotten to put away groceries until the ice cream becomes soup.)

I know, I know, I still haven't explained why Dawn doesn't live down the hall from me anymore. Here's the story: First of all, even before Sharon and my dad married, Jeff (Dawn's brother) had realized that he would never enjoy living in Connecticut. He missed his dad and he missed California, so the only solution was for him to move back out there. Naturally, Dawn missed him and her dad like crazy, which meant that she ended up being bicoastal for a while. (That's just a fancy way of saying that she spent a lot of time in the air, flying between the East and West Coasts.) After awhile her visits west lasted longer and longer, and finally, she decided California was her real home, and she moved there permanently. She still visits here, of course, but I doubt she'll ever live in Connecticut again.

And I doubt I'll ever really be used to her not being here.

It's hard to return to living as an only child once you've had a sister around. Even though

5

I have another best friend (her name's Kristy Thomas), I know nobody will ever replace Dawn in my heart.

I know that Sharon misses Dawn a whole lot, too. I could see it in her eyes when I entered the kitchen for breakfast. For just a fraction of a second, I could see her looking past me, as if she hoped that somehow Dawn had followed me down the stairs. There was a sudden sadness in her eyes, and then, just as suddenly, it was gone. I gave her a special smile and a quick hug, trying to put everything I felt into it and yet keep it casual. She hugged me back, and I had a feeling she'd taken in every message I'd been trying to send her. Sharon and I are pretty sensitive people, and both of us are good at sending and receiving those unspoken communications.

"Morning, Dad," I said, kissing the top of my father's head as I walked past him toward the cupboard where we keep the cereal. He was reading the *Stoneybrook News* and eating a buttered cinnamon-raisin bagel; he looked up briefly and gave me a smile before he returned to his reading.

I filled a bowl with Grape Nuts, added skim milk and a little maple syrup, poured a glass of orange juice, and sat at the table. Before we moved into this old farmhouse with Sharon and Dawn, my dad and I used to eat very differently. For breakfast, we'd have eggs and bacon. Lunches, when we were both home, usually involved cold cuts from the local deli. And we often had burgers or pork chops for dinner. But all that changed when we married into a health-conscious family. Now we eat a mostly vegetarian diet, and while you can't make me like tofu, I will say that I don't miss red meat all that much. (Of course, my dad and I still sneak in the occasional T-bone, when we can.)

I was crunching away contentedly on my Grape Nuts when I heard my dad make a "tsk-tsk" sound. I looked up to see him shaking his head over something he was reading in the paper.

"That's a real shame," he said.

"What is?" I asked.

"Fowler's latest project," he answered.

"Ugh, that *man!*" exclaimed Sharon, making a face. She can't stand hearing about Reginald Fowler. He's this very rich, very flashy guy who made his money, as she says, by "selling off Stoneybrook, tree by tree." He's a developer, and it's true that he's changed the face of our town by putting up strip malls where there used to be fields, and office buildings where forests once stood. I don't like Fowler much, myself. I'd rather have Stoneybrook the way it was when I was little, when it looked more like an old-fashioned small town.

"What's he up to now?" I asked.

"He wants to build a huge new office complex," my dad replied. "He says it'll bring thousands of jobs to the area."

"More likely it'll put thousands of dollars into his pocket," said Sharon, with a little snort.

"Where does he want to build it?" I asked.

"On the land where Ambrose's Sawmill stands," said my dad. "You know, Miller's Park?"

"That's *awful!*" I exploded, putting down my spoon so suddenly that milk droplets flew all over the table. "Miller's Park is so beautiful." I thought of the little stream that curves through the park, which is on the outskirts of town, and of the weeping willows that line the stream's banks.

"And the Historical Society just spent all that time raising money to renovate Ambrose's Sawmill," Sharon added. "How dare he?"

My dad shrugged. "So far it's just a proposal," he said. "Maybe it won't go through. He'll have to take it to the town council, first. But Fowler is a powerful man. I wouldn't be too surprised if that sawmill is torn down within a month or two."

He read a little further. "*This* is interesting," he said. "It says here that there was a mysterious fire at one of the houses that sit on the edge of that land — one of the houses that Fowler would have to buy and knock down before he started his project."

"I bet Fowler set it!" said Sharon.

"Now, now, that hasn't been proven," said my father. "But it does say here that the fire inspectors haven't ruled out arson." He began reading the paper again, and I continued to eat breakfast, and think about how sad it would be to lose those weeping willows.

I finished my Grape Nuts without really tasting them, rinsed out the bowl and stuck it into the dishwasher, and kissed my dad and Sharon good-bye. Fowler or not, it was time to leave for school.

As usual, my friends Stacey McGill and Mallory Pike stopped by for me. Then we headed for school, meeting Claudia, Jessi, and Logan on the way. Guess what we talked about on the way to school? No, not the BSC, although we are all members and we often do talk about club business during our walk.

What we talked about was Fowler's plans and how to fight them. That's what I love about my friends. They, like me, believe in doing something to help whenever help is needed. No sooner had we started on the topic of the threat to Miller's Park than we were planning a campaign of letters to the editor.

"We'd better begin soon, too," said Jessi. "I have a feeling this fight isn't going to be an easy one."

As it turned out, Jessi couldn't have been more right. The BSC versus Reginald Fowler turned out to be one of our toughest fights ever.

CHAPTER 2

"Why stop at letters to the editor? We should pull together a whole media campaign. Maybe the TV news people would be interested!" Kristy was talking fast, the way she always does when she knows she has a good idea, and her face was a little flushed.

I know that face well. Kristy Thomas and I have been best friends forever, and I've seen Kristy come up with lots of good ideas. The best one, so far anyway, was her idea for the BSC. We were in the midst of a BSC meeting that Monday afternoon, and while we waited for phone calls we discussed the Fowler problem.

The BSC began back in seventh grade, when Kristy had a major brainstorm. She realized, while watching her mom try to find a sitter for Kristy's little brother, that parents would give anything to have a simple way to arrange for baby-sitters. Ever since then the BSC (with

Kristy as president, naturally) has been meeting in Claudia's room every Monday, Wednesday, and Friday afternoon from five-thirty until six. When parents call during those times, they are virtually guaranteed a responsible, reliable, experienced sitter.

But the BSC isn't only about making life easier for parents. We really care about kids; we write up all our jobs in the club notebook, so that every sitter knows what's going on with every child. We also help our charges have fun; we all own and often carry Kid-Kits, which are boxes full of stickers, art supplies, and hand-me-down toys that kids just love. Lastly, the BSC is super-organized; the club record book contains detailed notes on every client — name, address, allergies, likes and dislikes — as well as information about every sitter's schedule.

In case you're wondering, all of the above are products of Kristy's Brilliant Brain, which never seems to stop working, just like the rest of her. Kristy's always on the go, and always diving into things headfirst. Sometimes I'm amazed that we're best friends; we are as different as night and day. We do look alike — both of us have brown hair and brown eyes, and we're on the short side — but as far as personality goes, we're opposites. Remember

I told you I am shy and sensitive? Kristy is anything but.

I wonder if it has to do partly with our family lives. For most of my life I was an only child with one parent, and I always received plenty of attention. In fact, more than I wanted. But Kristy grew up in a chaotic household, with two older brothers (Charlie and Sam) and one younger one (David Michael), all of whom shared one parent: Kristy's mom (her dad walked out on the family when David Michael was only a baby). If Kristy wanted attention, she had to *work* for it. That was always the case, and it still is, maybe now more than ever. See, Kristy's mother is married again, to a great guy named Watson Brewer, who just happens to be a millionaire. Kristy and her mom and her brothers moved across town to live in his mansion, which they also share (every other month) with Watson's children from his first marriage, Karen and Andrew. Watson and Kristy's mom also adopted a little Vietnamese girl, Emily Michelle, and soon after she arrived, Kristy's grandmother Nannie moved in to help out. It's a pretty full house (mansion, that is), even if you don't count the animals! Kristy seems to thrive on the atmosphere there, and even seeks out more chaos. For example, she coaches a softball team for little kids, called Kristy's Krushers. And, as she was demonstrating during our meeting that afternoon, she's always on the alert for new problems to be solved, new ventures to begin, and new fights to be fought.

". . . and maybe we should organize some kind of protest or rally," she was saying, still champing at the bit to wage the war on Fowler.

"Come on, Kristy, chill!" said Claudia, passing her a bag of jelly beans. "I mean, everything you're saying sounds great, but we can't do it all at once. Let's start small and move on from there." Claud reached up to check that her ponytail was still on top of her head, Pebbles-style.

Claudia Kishi, who is vice-president of the BSC (mainly because she has her own phone, with a private line), is Japanese-American, with long, jet-black hair and almond-shaped eyes. I've known her all my life, but I'm sometimes still amazed at how beautiful she is.

Here are Claudia's three main passions: art, art, and art.

Not really. I mean, art is very important to Claudia, but it's not the only thing in her life. For example, she's also passionate about clothes (she believes that you are what you wear), junk food (she lives on the stuff, and provides munchies for every BSC meeting), and Nancy Drew mysteries (Claudia's a terrific

14

detective herself). Her parents disapprove of the junk food and the mysteries, so Claudia's become a master of deception, hiding books, candy, and chips in every little nook and cranny of her room.

Claudia is *not* passionate about school. She makes good grades in art class, but that's about it. She's not dumb. She just doesn't care much about dates and numbers and the exact way to spell things. Her older sister Janine does, though. Janine's a true genius who takes college classes even though she's still in high school. Fortunately, Claudia's parents have begun to value Claud's creative abilities as much as Janine's academic talents.

Claudia's best friend, Stacey McGill, who was sitting next to Claudia on the bed that afternoon, spoke up next. "I agree with Claudia," she said. "Let's begin with letters to the editor and see what happens next. Meanwhile, I think there's a little piece of business we're forgetting today!" She said that last part in a teasing voice, holding up a manila envelope as she spoke.

We all groaned. "That's right," said Stacey. "It's dues day. Pay up, everybody." She smiled around at us, ignoring our grumbling. Stacey is the treasurer of the BSC, and math whiz that she is, she does a great job. Although we each keep the money we make

15

from sitting jobs, we do contribute a small amount to the club fund every week, just to cover expenses such as Claudia's phone bill. It's no big deal, really. We just like to give Stacey a hard time about it.

Stacey, who has blonde hair (usually in a wildly curly perm) and blue eyes, is an only child who lives with her mom. Her parents are divorced, and her dad lives in Manhattan, where Stacey grew up. And, while Stacey chose to live in Stoneybrook with her mom, she'll never really be a small-town girl. She's a city person, and always will be, no matter where she lives. Stacey has a certain sophistication — partly reflected in her excellent taste in clothes — that stands out in Stoneybrook.

She's not a snob, though. Oh, she went through a period not long ago when she decided that the members of the BSC were too "immature" to hang out with, but that didn't last long. She found out who her real friends were, and now she's back in the club, where she belongs. I'm glad, too. I hated it when we were all mad at her.

Stacey's a diabetic, which I think gives her a certain perspective on life. That is, she doesn't take it for granted. Diabetes is a serious, lifelong disease. Stacey's body doesn't process sugars correctly, which means that she has to be very, very careful about what she eats, and must give herself shots of insulin, which her body needs but doesn't produce.

We all paid our dues, and just as Stacey was closing the envelope, the phone rang. Kristy grabbed it. "Hello, Baby-sitters Club," she said. She listened for a few minutes, making little "mmm-hmm" noises, and then hung up, after promising she'd call right back.

"That was a new client," she explained with a smile. Kristy loves new clients. Hearing from them proves, according to her, that the BSC receives great word-of-mouth advertising from our regular clients. We used to advertise a lot, with fliers, but we find we don't need to much anymore. "Her name's Mrs. Martinez," Kristy continued. "She teaches science at the high school, and so does her husband. They're in a bind because their regular sitter just quit, and they need someone to watch their kids every afternoon — starting tomorrow — until they can find a new one." Kristy turned to me. "Is there any way we can take on a commitment like that?" she asked.

I pulled the record book onto my lap and opened it. I'm the club secretary, and I pride myself on my neat, accurate record-keeping. I can see at a glance which of us is available for any particular job, and let me tell you, keeping track of all our schedules is not easy. "Hmmm, doesn't look good," I said. "Nobody has every

17

single afternoon free. But if we each take a few afternoons here and there, we could do it. I can take the first shift tomorrow."

"I'm sure Mrs. Martinez wouldn't mind, as long as the hours are covered," said Kristy, reaching for the phone. She talked to Mrs. Martinez for a few minutes, then hung up, looking surprised. "She says that'll be fine," she informed us. "But listen to what else she told me. Mrs. Martinez says that their house is a bit of a mess. They just had a small fire, and she says things are still a little smoky and smelly. Guess where they live."

I knew right away. "Near Miller's Park?" I asked. Kristy nodded. "Theirs must be the house that the paper mentioned this morning. The one that Fowler needs to buy in order to develop Miller's Park!"

"Isn't that the most amazing coincidence?" Kristy marveled. "Here we were, just talking about what's happening over there, and she calls."

"I may have to put off sitting for the Martinezes until they have things cleaned up," said Abby. "That smoke might make my allergies kick into high gear."

Abby Stevenson is the newest member of the BSC. She was invited to join after Dawn moved back to California, and she's taken over Dawn's position in the club, which is alternate officer. That just means she fills in for any of the other officers who might be absent from a meeting.

While Abby has taken Dawn's position, she can never exactly take her place. I like Abby a lot — we all do — but she and Dawn are very different. Abby just moved here from Long Island, which is about as much on the East Coast as you can be, while Dawn will always love California. And Abby is full of energy and rushes into things, while Dawn is more laid-back.

Abby is an identical twin. Her sister's name is Anna. I don't know Anna too well yet, but I do know that she's an amazing musician. She plays violin on practically a professional level. Abby, meanwhile, loves sports and almost any kind of physical activity. She runs, she plays soccer, she skis. And she does it all despite the fact that she's allergic to just about *everything*. As if that weren't enough, she also has asthma.

Abby and Anna live in Kristy's neighborhood with their mom, who commutes to work in New York City. Their dad died in a car wreck a few years ago. Abby never talks about that, but I can tell that his death affected her in some really major ways. Maybe it's just that I can identify with her, since I'm what I call a "half-orphan," too.

Since no other phone calls came in for a few minutes, we started to talk about the new clients. "How old are the kids?" asked Mallory. Kristy told her the Martinezes have an eight-year-old boy and a three-year-old girl. "Maybe Nicky knows the boy from school," said Mal.

Mallory Pike and her best friend Jessica Ramsey are the club's junior officers, which means that since they're eleven and in the sixth grade (unlike the rest of us, who are all thirteen and in the eighth grade), they aren't allowed to sit at night unless it's for their own families. They take care of a lot of our afternoon jobs.

It was a good bet that Mal would have a sister or brother to match the new kids' ages. She has seven younger siblings, including a set of identical triplets. If you ask her, she can say all of their names in one breath, like this: "ByronAdamJordanVanessaNickyMargoClaire!" The Pike kids are a handful, no doubt about it. Mal has had a lot of sitting experience for someone her age.

Mal is white, with reddish-brown hair, glasses, and braces. She's cute now, and she's going to be really pretty someday, but she doesn't believe that. She's smart, too, and a good artist and writer. When she grows up she wants to be an author and illustrator of children's books.

Jessi has a smaller family. She lives with her parents, her little sister Becca, her baby brother Squirt (real name: John Philip Ramsey, Jr.), and her Aunt Cecelia. Jessi is African-American, and has cocoa-brown skin, deep velvety brown eyes, and legs that seem to go on forever. She's a serious ballet student and an incredible dancer.

There are two more members of the BSC, but neither of them said anything that afternoon, for the very simple reason that neither of them was at the meeting. They're both associate members, which means that they help out when we have more jobs than we can handle. One of them happens to be Logan. The other is Shannon Kilbourne, who lives in Kristy's and Abby's neighborhood but who goes to a private school called Stoneybrook Day School. She's super-smart, pretty, and fun to be around.

Our meeting wound up soon after Mrs. Martinez's call. I was excited about having new clients, especially because I would be the first to sit for them. And I was glad they lived near Miller's Park, if only because I wanted to spend some time there before Fowler destroyed it. I knew that might happen, even if the BSC did everything we could to stop him. We're the best baby-sitters in Stoneybrook, but I had to admit that wouldn't mean anything when it came to fighting Reginald Fowler.

CHAPTER 3

"I know, the odor is awful. We've had the windows open forever, but it still smells." Mrs. Martinez was showing me where the fire had started, in the garage, and she'd noticed me wrinkling my nose at the acrid smell of smoke that hung in the air.

It was Tuesday afternoon, and I had just met Mrs. Martinez and her two children: Luke, the eight-year-old, and Amalia, who is three. All three of them had dark hair, dark eyes, and infectious smiles. I liked them already. Their house was small and cozy, and fortunately had not been severely damaged in the fire. The garage was going to need a lot of work, and they'd lost practically everything that had been stored there, but it was the only place where you could see the effects of the fire. The smell, on the other hand, pervaded the entire house.

"How did the fire start?" I asked Mrs. Mar-

23

tinez as we headed back into the house.

I could hear snatches of the "Circle of Life" song as we sat in the kitchen, talking. Mrs. Martinez had brought home a *Lion King* sing-along video and was letting the kids watch it so that she and I would be able to talk uninterrupted. "This being the first time you're here, and all," she'd explained. I was glad she wasn't the type to run off after a hurried hello. I think it's important to take the time to talk with new clients and learn a little about their kids, their schedules, and what kind of household rules the family has. Mrs. Martinez seemed to feel the same way. She'd arranged to stay home for a half hour after I'd arrived.

"We still don't know how the fire started," she answered. "All we know is that it began in the garage. Fortunately, our baby-sitter at the time smelled the smoke and was able to move the kids out of the house. Luke ran across the street and told the neighbors, who called the fire department. They showed up quickly. The garage door was open, so they charged in and put the fire out before it could spread into the house."

"That's great," I said.

"It sure is. We were so lucky," said Mrs. Martinez. She sighed. "It's going to be a while before we have things back in order, though. My husband and I are both so busy. We run an after-school tutoring program at the high school, and we both teach adult education classes in the evenings. That's why we need a sitter every day. We're so glad your club could fill in; we thought we were done for when our other sitter told us she had to quit."

"Well, I'm glad we could help," I said. "Personally, I love this neighborhood. Miller's Park is so pretty! I'll be glad to sit for you whenever I can."

"We love Miller's Park, too," said Mrs. Martinez. "And Ambrose's Sawmill. I'd hate to see it destroyed."

I nodded. "So you won't sell out to Fowler?" I asked.

"Never!" she replied. "We've worked too hard for this house. We would never give it up and start all over again." She shook her head. "I can't stand the arrogance of that rich developer. He thinks he can just waltz in here and do anything he likes to Stoneybrook. Well, he'll find out just how wrong he is. Not everybody can be bought."

She sounded angry, and I didn't blame her. After all, who was Fowler? Some guy who thought he could make a lot of money by ruining our town. I was glad to know that the Martinezes were going to stand up to him.

Mrs. Martinez showed me around the

kitchen, and pointed out a list of emergency phone numbers she'd posted on a bulletin board by the phone. Then she said good-bye to the kids, gave me a few last-minute instructions on afternoon snacks, and headed off.

"Hey, Luke. Hey, Amalia," I said, joining them in the living room as their video ended. "What would you guys like to do now?" It was time to become acquainted with my new charges.

"Polly Pocket?" Amalia asked hopefully, holding up a tiny doll. She had crawled onto my lap the second I sat down. I smiled at her. She was very affectionate.

Luke rolled his eyes. "No way am I playing with that dumb doll," he protested, more to Amalia than to me. So far he hadn't met my eyes once or talked directly to me. I figured he was shy, which I could relate to. I decided to give him space and hope he'd eventually become more friendly.

"Tell you what," I said. "How about if we have a quick snack, and then go outside and explore Miller's Park for a while?"

Amalia agreed happily, once I'd said it was fine with me if she brought Polly Pocket. Luke didn't seem as enthusiastic, but he said that if I was going, he'd go.

I told them I was going to put together their snack, and that I'd be right back. Amalia curled up in the corner of the couch, crooning to her doll. But Luke followed me into the kitchen. I smiled to myself. Maybe he was already losing his shyness. "Want to pour out some juice for everybody?" I asked him.

"Okay," he mumbled, looking down at his sneakers. He still wasn't acting too friendly, but he did seem to want to stay close by me. I was a little confused by his behavior, but I tried not to let it bother me. Every kid is different, and as an experienced sitter I've learned to accept those differences and enjoy them.

I wondered what it would take to reach him, to make friends with him. I decided to try flattery. "I hear you were really brave, the way you ran across the street for help on the day of the fire," I said as I spread cream cheese onto a bagel for Amalia.

"How did you know about that?" he asked, sounding angry. He was looking directly at me for the first time.

"Um, your mom told me," I answered.

"Yeah? What else did she say?"

"Just that you all were able to leave the house safely," I replied lamely. Something about Luke's attitude didn't seem quite right. Why was he so defensive about the fire? "That must have been a scary day," I continued, trying to sound neutral.

"It was no big deal," he said, staring at his sneakers again.

"Were you the first one to smell smoke, or was it your baby-sitter?" I asked, more to keep him talking than because I was interested.

"I don't know," he answered quickly. "I really don't remember much about that day, okay?" He returned the juice carton to the refrigerator and closed the door — hard.

"Okay," I said. It sounded as if Luke knew — and remembered — more than he was letting on. But if he didn't want to talk about it, I wasn't about to force him. After all, I wanted to make friends with him, and I hoped we could both enjoy the time we'd be spending together. I didn't want him to feel angry at me, or on the spot. "Would you go tell Amalia that the snack is ready?" I asked.

"You come, too," he insisted.

What was going on here? Luke didn't want to let me out of his sight, that was obvious. But why? I knew it wasn't because I had suddenly become his favorite person in the world. I wondered if the fire had been so traumatic that he was now afraid to be alone. Or maybe he'd always been that way. In any case, I decided not to make waves. "Okay," I agreed. "We'll both go tell her."

Half an hour later, when we'd finished eating and cleaning up, the three of us headed outside. It was a warm spring afternoon, and everywhere we looked we saw trees budding, daffodils blooming, and birds singing. The sun was so warm that I took off my sweatshirt and tied it around my waist. Amalia ran ahead, picking dandelions and carrying them back to me. Luke dawdled, staying close behind me and ignoring most of my comments.

Miller's Park is a beautiful, peaceful place. There's all sorts of history attached to it, too, but I can never remember the details. All I know is that there's a stream running through the grounds, and that at this time of year purple violets bloomed beneath the weeping willows. We saw a robin bringing a worm to its nest, and a squirrel digging for nuts, and a duck swimming around on the millpond, acting as if it owned the place.

We poked around Ambrose's Sawmill, and I read out loud from the sign posted in front of it telling about the planned renovations. The Historical Society had big plans for the site. I felt angry all over again when I thought about Reginald Fowler knocking the place down. Not to mention bulldozing the whole park. I mean, where would the robins and squirrels and ducks go? Didn't he *care*?

I kept most of my feelings to myself, though. Amalia wouldn't have understood anyway, and I didn't want to be negative around Luke.

I was still hoping he'd open up a little more. He did seem to enjoy our walk in the park, but while he never strayed far from my side, he didn't talk much, either.

The same was true when we found ourselves back at the house.

On the way inside, Luke had opened the mailbox and retrieved the day's mail. He stood in the hall leafing through it while I helped Amalia out of her jacket. At one point, he glanced up to see if I was watching, and I looked away quickly. But I turned back in time to see him pull a sheet of paper out of an envelope, read it quickly, then tear it into pieces and throw the scraps into a trash basket beneath the hall table.

Now I was really curious.

But it took the rest of the afternoon before I could satisfy my curiosity, because Luke never left my side. Finally, when he went to the bathroom at one point, I made a dash for the trash basket, grabbed the pieces of paper, and tucked them into my pocket.

Later that night, when I returned home, I pulled them out. Unfortunately, I hadn't been able to grab all the pieces. I could see that there was printing on the note, in large, dark capital letters. But the only words I could read were these: "IF YOU" and "YOU WILL BE."

What did it mean? There was something strange going on at the Martinez house. I had a feeling that Luke knew something about it, too, but he wasn't talking. I was going to have to find out for myself.

CHAPTER 4

I couldn't wait to tell my friends about Luke's strange behavior, and the torn-up note. Both things seemed pretty mysterious, and if there's one thing everyone in the BSC loves, it's a mystery. But, as it turned out, I came very close to forgetting about my sitting job with the Martinezes. Why? Well, because something much more exciting happened the next day.

It all started when I came down to breakfast on Wednesday morning. Sharon smiled at me when I walked into the kitchen, and started applauding. Then my dad joined in. "There she is," exclaimed Sharon. "Our own young celebrity! We're proud of you, honey." She gave me a hug.

I rubbed my eyes. I had no idea what they were talking about. For a second I thought I wasn't really awake yet, and that this was all a weird dream. But after I'd rubbed my eyes,

I found I was still standing in the middle of the kitchen, and Sharon and my dad were both still smiling at me. "Um, what are you guys talking about?" I asked. "Did I win an Oscar or something?"

"You don't know?" asked my dad.

"Show her! Show her!" cried Sharon. She grabbed the newspaper and, folding it back to the editorial page, handed it over to me.

I took a glance, and nearly passed out. There was my name, in the middle of the page, beneath the letter I'd written on Monday after our BSC meeting. "Mary Anne Spier, Secretary, Baby-sitters Club," it said, right there in black and white. (Kristy had convinced us that using our BSC titles would be "more impressive.") And there was Kristy's name and title, and Stacey's. In fact, every one of the letters that the BSC members had written to the editor of the *Stoneybrook News* had been printed. They were grouped together, under a big headline that read CONCERNED YOUTH TAKE ON DEVELOPER. "Wow," I breathed. "That was quick. Claudia took those letters down to the newspaper office only yesterday." I felt sort of queasy. I mean, I'd written my letter because I believed the issue deserved attention, and I had been proud to sign my name. But seeing it there in print made me feel a little exposed.

"Well, the editor seems to have a pretty

strong opinion about the issue," my dad remarked. He pointed to a column that ran down the side of the page. It was titled IDE-ALISTS? PERHAPS. BUT THEY HAVE THE RIGHT IDEA. I started to read it out loud. " 'Many of our readers may glance at the letters on this page and dismiss them as the work of a bunch of naive, idealistic kids,' " I read. " 'I'll admit that that was my first impulse, when they arrived in my office. But the more I thought about it, the more I realized that these kids had a point. The world — and Stoneybrook — really does not need another office park. What this town *does* need are beautiful spaces where people can gather and be comfortable. Spaces where they can sit in the sun, walk their dogs, play catch, eat a picnic lunch. Spaces where they can reaffirm their sense of community, and their sense of that community's history. Miller's Park can be, and should be, such a space. The kids have the right idea.' " The editorial went on, but I skipped over to an article on the facing page.

A reporter had interviewed Reginald Fowler, giving him the chance to react to our letters. As you can imagine, his reaction was not good. He wasn't at all pleased with what he called the "uninformed opinions" of the BSC members. He also said he had no intention of giving up his plans for what he called "Carter

Park," which I thought was strange. I'd never heard it called that before. And he mentioned an upcoming town council meeting at which everything would be decided, once and for all. The meeting was a couple of weeks away.

"Wow!" I exclaimed, putting down the paper. It looked as if our letters had started something. Something big.

Sure enough, the word had spread all over school by lunchtime. The BSC was big news that day. Most of the kids — and teachers — who told us they'd seen our letters agreed with us, but not all. Some thought we were being ridiculous to suggest that saving "a couple of acres of weedy dirt" was important. We spent our whole lunch hour defending our viewpoint against a few kids who disagreed with us, and encouraging the ones who agreed to write their own letters.

When we left school that day, we discovered that the quarrel between the BSC and Fowler had hit the big time: it was in the Stamford papers. (Stamford is the city closest to Stoneybrook.) DEVELOPER FEUDS WITH LOCAL TEENS, said the headline in one paper. TEENS SPEAK OUT AGAINST PROJECT, announced another. The editor of one paper supported us, while the other paper's editor supported Fowler.

Kristy was beside herself. She barely remembered to call our meeting to order that afternoon, she was so excited. "This is the best publicity the club has had in a long time!" she crowed.

"Kristy," Stacey chided her gently, shaking her head. "Aren't you forgetting something? This isn't about the BSC. This is about Miller's Park."

"Right, right," said Kristy, chomping a handful of Cracker Jacks, which Claudia had passed to her. "I mean, I know that. I haven't forgotten what's really important here. But you have to admit, it *is* great publicity."

Kristy adores publicity. She was positively glowing as we talked about our next move in the war against Fowler. She wanted to call a press conference.

Mallory thought a demonstration might be a good idea.

Stacey wanted to start calling all the local politicians.

Claudia (naturally) was dying to design a poster we could plaster all over town.

Abby came up with the idea of challenging Fowler to a public debate.

I didn't mind that idea, as long as I didn't have to be onstage. I also thought we should make sure the Historical Society was involved in whatever we did, since they had a real stake in the survival of Miller's Park and Ambrose's Sawmill.

Logan, who had come to the meeting that day, thought that the club should support the Martinezes in their fight against Fowler. "They're such nice people," he said. He had just come from sitting for Luke and Amalia. I didn't have a chance to ask whether he'd noticed Luke acting strangely.

We decided, after talking about the options, that for now we would concentrate on what Kristy called a "letter blitz." We'd keep writing letters to the editor, and we hoped that other people would join in and write letters, too. "Public opinion is the most important thing," said Kristy. "Once he sees that everyone is against him, Fowler will probably just give up and crawl away with his tail between his legs."

At the time, I thought Kristy was right. But over the next couple of days, as more and more letters and articles appeared in the paper, it became clear that Fowler was not going to be crawling away anytime soon.

Dear Editor,
I am a fourth-grader at SES, and I have always loved Miller's Park. I think Mr. Fowler is a

very bad man. Or at least he has bad ideas. Please don't ruin our park, Mr. Fowler!

Sincerely, Tiffany Spencer

Dear Editor,
I have lived in Stoneybrook all my life, and I believe that Miller's Park is an important and beautiful place for all the children and adults in this town. . . .

Sincerely, Claudia Lynn Kishi

Dear Editor,
I am writing as president of the Stoneybrook Historical Society and as a citizen of Stoneybrook. Miller's Park is one of our town's most valuable assets. I join the members of the Baby-sitters Club and others in condemning Mr. Fowler's plans. . . .

Sincerely, Jane Kellogg

Dear Editor,
As a small-business owner and a member in good standing of the Stoneybrook Rotary Club, I feel I must write to express my disgust with the current brouhaha over the development of Miller's Park. Those who protest that it must be saved may be sweet, well-meaning

children, but they clearly have no understanding of economics. . . .

Sincerely, Don Parker

Dear Editor,
I am an eighty-nine-year-old woman who grew up in Stoneybrook, and I have many sweet memories of time spent in Miller's Park. I support these wonderful kids who are trying to save it. Shame on you for ignoring their pleas, Mr. Fowler!

Sincerely, Berta Frank

DEVELOPER VOWS TO CONTINUE FIGHT
STONEYBROOK — Developer Reginald Fowler called a press conference today and renewed what he calls his "promise to Stoneybrook's business community." . . . The conference was interrupted several times by protesters who chanted, "People, Not Profits!" Fowler responded angrily to the protest and assured reporters and the public that he had Stoneybrook's "best interests at heart." . . .

Dear Editor,
I am writing again to say that, although my friends and I are young, we believe we know

more about Stoneybrook's "best interests" than Mr. Fowler does. . . .

> Sincerely, Kristin Amanda Thomas

ARE YOUNG PROTESTERS IN OVER THEIR HEADS?

A guest editorial by Samuel Dodds, President of Dodds Management Corp.

Since when do we let public policy be decided by children? Clearly, the controversy over Miller's Park has struck a chord. Unfortunately, most of those who object to its development as an office park are short-sighted, naive, and completely uninformed regarding the incredible prosperity such development could bring to Stoneybrook. . . .

Dear Editor,
Is it short-sighted to believe in preserving history? Is it naive to distrust wealthy developers? If so, I am happy to be called by those names. . . .

> Sincerely, Mary Anne Spier

CHAPTER 5

The afternoon started off so innocently. It's still hard for me to believe how it all ended up. Mary Anne Spier, Suspected Criminal. I wonder if this is going to end up on my permanent record somewhere.

Oh, don't worry. I didn't really do anything. But it sure did look bad. I guess I should start from the beginning, so here goes.

It was a Tuesday afternoon, and I was sitting for Luke and Amalia. I was a little frustrated because, so far, I hadn't made much headway with Luke. He still stuck by my side like glue, but he wasn't exactly friendly. It was almost as if he were suspicious of *me*! Ridiculous, I know, but that's how it seemed. Amalia, on the other hand, had continued to be one of the most affectionate little kids I'd ever met.

When I arrived at the Martinezes', Amalia ran to greet me with a big hug, a loud, wet kiss on the cheek, and a whispered "I love you." She was irresistible. She had no trouble talking me into helping her cut out some paper dolls while she crayoned new dresses for them. (She didn't stay in the lines much, but her scrawls were colorful.) Luke brought his math homework into the rec room where we were playing and sat at a desk in the corner, as if he wanted to keep an eye on us.

"Look at this dress!" Amalia said, holding up one she'd just finished.

"Pretty," I remarked. Amalia flashed me a big smile.

"Can you cut me another doll, pretty please, Allie?" she asked.

"Sure," I replied, "but my name's Mary Anne." I noticed Luke shooting a nasty look at Amalia, as if he thought she was unbelievably dumb for forgetting my name. It didn't bother me. I've had kids call me everything from "Mom" to "Kristy." When they're excited, sometimes they just forget who they're talking to. I picked up the scissors and started to cut out the doll Amalia had asked for.

"Mary Anne," Amalia repeated agreeably. "Mary Anne, Fairy Anne, Carry Anne, Beary Anne," she sang beneath her breath as she continued to color. I smiled to myself.

"Gary Dan, Sary Man, Lary Ban," Amalia continued, a little louder.

"Amalia!" Luke sounded annoyed. "Cut it out."

"Stary Gan, Wary Tan," Amalia chanted, clearly enjoying herself.

"Amalia," Luke repeated, in a warning tone.

"If it's bothering you, you could always work in the kitchen," I suggested. Luke didn't seem to like that idea. He frowned at Amalia, clapped his hands over his ears, and returned to his math homework.

Just then, the phone rang. Luke and I both jumped up to answer it. "I'll get it," he said.

"It's the sitter's job to answer the phone," I told him. "I'll answer it." I left the room, noticing that for once he didn't follow me. I answered the phone, took a message for Mr. Martinez, and headed back to the rec room. As I came through the door, I saw Luke jump up from the couch and race back to his seat at the desk.

When I glanced at the couch, I saw my backpack sitting there. At first I thought it was just as I'd left it, but when I came closer I could tell that the top zipper had been opened. It looked as if someone had been rummaging through my stuff.

I glanced at Luke. He appeared to be deep

in thought, leaning over his math book with a wrinkled brow. I took a breath, opened my mouth, and was about to say something when, suddenly, I had second thoughts. After all, I could see that nothing had disappeared from my backpack. And there was a slight possibility that I'd left it open that way and just forgotten. There was no point in accusing Luke, possibly unfairly, of snooping through my things. He wasn't crazy about me as it was, and I didn't want to make things any worse.

I snapped my mouth shut and gazed around the room. When my eye lit on a shelf full of board games, I had an inspiration. "Hey, Luke," I said. "How about a game of checkers? Me and Amalia against you, okay?"

Luke looked up at me, and I thought I saw relief in his eyes. "Um, sure," he agreed. "I'm all done with my homework, anyway. I'll set it up."

"I'm on *your* team," said Amalia, climbing into my lap and smiling up at me. "We can win him, right?"

"Sure we can," I replied, returning the smile.

"I wouldn't be so sure," said Luke, who had brought the board over to the coffee table. "I'm the checkers champion of our family, you know." He gave me a quick grin.

"Really?" I asked. "Cool!"

After a few minutes, it was clear that Luke really was good at checkers. I had to focus all my attention on what was happening on the board, and even so he was soon winning easily. He had about six kings, and Amalia and I didn't have even one. I took my time with my turns, trying hard to figure out a good strategy. Finally, I was able to move one of my pieces to the back row. "King me!" I cried triumphantly.

When Luke didn't respond, I looked up from the board and found him staring over my shoulder at something behind me. His face was white and his mouth was open. He looked terrified.

I turned around quickly — and caught a glimpse of a figure darting away, just outside the window. It was hard to see clearly, because the window was one near the garage, and it was still dirty with soot from the fire. But the soot didn't cover the whole window. Instead, there were strange marks in the soot, marks that almost looked like writing.

I stood up and walked over to the window. Luke joined me. As soon as I was closer, I could see that the marks *were* writing. Writing that said:

DON'T TELL

"Don't tell?" I asked. "What does that mean? Don't tell what? Who could have written that?" My voice was a little shaky.

Luke looked up at me, still white-faced. He didn't say a word.

I returned to the couch and picked up Amalia. "How about a little piggyback ride?" I asked her, trying to hide the fact that I was feeling totally creeped out.

"Yea!" she yelled, clambering onto my back.

"I'm going to take a closer look at that writing," I told Luke. He followed me outside, and we both walked around to inspect the window. Guess what? By the time we reached the window, the writing was gone — wiped away — and there was no sign of the writer, either. "Weird," I said. Once again, Luke didn't say anything.

I looked around and noticed that the sun had come out (it had been gray and drizzly when I'd arrived at the Martinezes'). "Let's stay outside for a while," I suggested. "How about if we take a walk?" I thought I'd keep a sharp eye out for any suspicious characters, and at the same time become acquainted with a neighborhood I hadn't spent much time in before. As usual, Luke seemed to be more than willing to stick with me, although the short burst of friendliness he'd shown during the

46

checkers game had disappeared. Amalia was happy as long as she had her piggyback ride, so we started walking around the block.

"Hey, there," the next-door neighbor greeted us as we walked by. He was working in his garden, but he stood up and brushed off his hands. He was a tall, thin, gray-haired man with piercing blue eyes. "I'm Mr. Fontecchio," he said. "You baby-sitting these kids?"

"That's right," I answered, thinking he was a little nosy. I decided not to offer my name. "Your daffodils are pretty," I added, to be polite.

"Sure, sure," he said. "But I'll be leaving them behind soon. As soon as Fowler hands over the bucks!" He laughed as he pulled a pipe out of his shirt pocket and lit it. Puffing away, he went on and on about how smart he and his two brothers had been to sell out to Fowler, and how ridiculous the Martinezes were being to hold out. "There's a bundle to be made!" he said.

"Uh-huh," I said, backing away. I thought he was a little strange. "Well, nice to meet you, Mr. Fontecchio." He gave me a little salute, and I headed off with Amalia on my back and Luke by my side.

Just then, a boy about Luke's age came running across the street.

"Hi, Steig," said Luke. "What's up?"

"Steig!" I heard a male voice call. "Where'd you go? I thought we were going to play catch." Then the owner of the voice appeared.

"Cary Retlin!" I exclaimed. "What are you doing here?" Cary Retlin is a boy I know from SMS. He moved to Stoneybrook just recently, but he already has a big reputation as a practical joker and a troublemaker. I was shocked to see him. And it wasn't exactly a happy surprise, since Cary and I haven't become friends. I don't trust him, to be frank.

"I live here," explained Cary. "Right across the street." He nodded at a small white house. "These are my brothers, Steig and Benson." He waved a hand at them. Benson, who had followed Cary across the street, looked about eleven. "Steig and Luke are best friends."

"Nice to meet you," I told them both.

Steig peered up at me. "Do you smoke?" he asked me.

"Uh, no," I replied. "I don't." I thought his question was awfully strange.

Cary seemed to think so, too. He gave me an apologetic shrug. Just then, I noticed a big black car cruising up the street, and I turned to make sure Luke and Steig weren't standing in the road. They weren't. They'd seen the car, too — and apparently something about it scared them. They both took off running, toward the woods in back of the Martinezes' house. Before I could even yell out their names, they'd disappeared.

"Oh, my lord!" I said. "I'm baby-sitting for Luke. I can't let him run off that way."

"We'll find them," said Cary. "Come on." After asking Benson to wait in the yard, he led me into the woods. I still had Amalia on my back, so I couldn't move too quickly, but I kept calling Luke's name and Cary kept calling Steig's. At one point, Cary held a tree branch so it wouldn't smack me as I passed, and I noticed soot on his hands. I was too upset to think much about it at the time, though.

Finally, as we were walking on a path near the edge of the woods, Steig reappeared. "Where's Luke?" I asked. He just shrugged, and I felt my stomach twist into a knot. Night was falling, and I had to find Luke as soon as possible. I hated to ask Cary for a favor, but there didn't seem to be any choice. "Cary," I said. "Can you watch Amalia for a few minutes so I can look for Luke?"

"Sure," he said. "We'll be back at my house." He helped Amalia, who was nearly asleep, off my back and onto his.

I set off, calling for Luke, running toward

Miller's Park and the old sawmill, the only area we hadn't checked yet. It was darker by then, and I was starting to feel a little creeped out about being alone in the woods. All was quiet, until, suddenly, I heard the unmistakable sound of glass breaking. I stopped in my tracks. Then I heard running footsteps. I quit calling for Luke and hid behind a tree, my heart beating hard. The footsteps passed very close to me, but I didn't dare to look. After they'd gone by, I came out from behind the tree and glanced down the path. At a distance, I could see two people talking. Curious, I tiptoed closer, hiding behind every convenient bush and tree along the way.

You'll never believe who I saw, there in a clearing in the woods. It was dusk and there was just enough light for me to be sure. Reginald Fowler, himself! He was talking to a teenaged boy, but I couldn't see the boy's face very clearly. The boy was bent over and breathing hard, which made me think he was the one I'd heard running. As I watched, Fowler passed the boy a wad of what looked like money. Then he and the boy took off, each in his own direction. The boy dropped something as he headed off.

I sneaked over and picked up the object he'd dropped. It was a brick — a brick with green paint on it. And as I looked at it, suddenly a bright light clicked on, shining into my eyes and blinding me.

"Freeze!" a loud male voice commanded. "Stoneybrook Police!"

CHAPTER 6

I did what he told me to do. I froze. Wouldn't you have? I went completely still, except for my hands, which were shaking. I didn't let go of the brick.

"Want to tell me what's going on here, young lady?" asked the voice.

I drew a deep, ragged breath. It took everything I had to resist the impulse to burst into tears. I tried to speak, but no words came out. I put up my hand to shield my eyes from the bright light, which was still shining on me. "I — I — could you turn that light off?" I don't know where I found the guts to ask him that, but I guess it was because I just couldn't take it any longer.

He didn't turn it off, but he stopped aiming it at my face. He came closer. "I'm Officer Cleary," he said. "Your name?"

For one wild second, I thought of giving him

a fake name. Hildegarde Braunschweiger. Annette Funicello. Jane Smith. Anything. But what came out was my real name. "Mary Anne Spier," I said meekly.

"And what are you doing in the woods?" he asked.

"I — I'm a baby-sitter," I explained. "I'm looking for one of my charges. He ran off."

The policeman, who looked as if he were about my father's age, nodded. He believed me! "How long ago was this?" he asked.

"I don't know," I said. I had lost all sense of time. "An hour?" Suddenly I remembered Amalia. Cary had promised to take care of her, but could I trust him? And where, oh where, was Luke? The Martinezes would be home soon — in fact, they might be home already. I started to panic. "I have to go!" I cried. "I have to check on the other child I was sitting for."

Officer Cleary nodded. "We can do that," he said. "But then you'll have to come down to the station with me."

"But — " I began.

He nodded toward the brick in my hand, and I looked down at it. A sick feeling washed over me. "I didn't — "

"Let's go," he said. "We can talk about it down at the station. First thing is to make sure those kids are okay." He held out his hand. At first I thought he wanted to shake, but then I realized he wanted me to give him the brick I was still holding. I handed it over. Then he led me to his squad car, which was parked near Ambrose's Sawmill, and introduced me to his partner, Officer Pelkey, who had been waiting in the car.

We drove straight to the Martinezes' (I was thankful that Officer Pelkey didn't feel a need to turn on the siren and the flashing lights), and Officer Cleary escorted me to the door.

Cary met us there. Who would ever have guessed I could be so glad to see Cary Retlin? When he saw Officer Cleary, he gave me a questioning glance, but I shook my head. "It's complicated," I said. "Where's Amalia? And what about Luke?"

"Luke came home on his own about twenty minutes ago," said Cary. "He and Amalia are in the kitchen, having a snack. They're both fine."

I breathed a huge sigh of relief. "I owe you one," I said.

"No problem," said Cary, smiling. Then his face changed. "Uh-oh," he said. He was looking past me.

"What?" I asked.

"I think Mrs. Martinez just came home," he answered.

I groaned. I didn't even have a chance to think about how to start explaining things before Mrs. Martinez ran into the house. "What is it?" she asked. "Why is that police car here? What's happened? Where are the kids?"

Officer Cleary stepped forward. "Mrs. Martinez?" he asked. She nodded. "Your kids are safe and sound. They're in the kitchen having a snack. But we have a problem here." Then he started to explain that he had found me in the woods after the police had received a report of suspicious activity in the vicinity. "There was some vandalism at Ambrose's Sawmill," he went on. "And this young lady here may have been involved. We're going to have to take her in for questioning."

"What?" said Mrs. Martinez. "You must be kidding. I don't know Mary Anne very well, but I do know one thing. She's no vandal. She's a decent, responsible girl."

My eyes welled up with tears. It felt so good to be defended, but I was so ashamed of what had happened. Even though it hadn't been my fault, I had done what no sitter should ever do: I had left my charges. And now I was in trouble with the law. I knew I'd be able to explain everything and clear my name — or at least I was pretty sure about that — but it was humiliating to have to stand there with Officer Cleary hovering over me. "I'm sorry, Mrs. Martinez," I said, trying to look her in the eyes. "I really am."

"Don't you worry, Mary Anne," she answered. "I know everything's going to work out just fine. I'll call your dad and tell him to meet you at the police station." She reached out and touched my hand. Then she hurried off to the kitchen to check on Luke and Amalia.

Cary gave me a little punch on the shoulder as he walked outside with Officer Cleary and me. "Hang in there," he said.

I felt the tears come again, and I ducked my head to hide them. "Thanks, Cary," I answered. "Thanks for everything." Maybe Cary Retlin wasn't so bad after all.

Officer Pelkey drove us downtown to the police station. When we walked in, my dad jumped up from a seat in the waiting area. "Mary Anne," he said, hugging me and stroking my hair. "Are you okay, sweetie?"

This time the tears came for real. I wiped them away. "Thanks for coming, Dad," I said. "I'm okay."

My father introduced himself to Officer Pelkey and Officer Cleary. "How about if I just take her home for now?" he asked. "I can bring her back tomorrow if you really need to see her."

Officer Cleary shook his head. "It would be really helpful for everyone involved if we could speak to her now," he said.

At that moment, a familiar figure came into the room. A tall, black-haired man, with sparkling blue eyes. "Sergeant Johnson!" I cried. I was so glad to see him. Sergeant Johnson is a good friend to the BSC. See, we've helped to solve more than one mystery in Stoneybrook, and Sergeant Johnson has been our main contact in the police department. By now, he knows we're good detectives, and he values our help.

"Mary Anne?" he said. "Mary Anne Spier? You're the one they were bringing in?" He shook his head. "Something's seriously cockeyed here."

Officer Cleary looked from me to Sergeant Johnson and back again. "You two know each other?" he asked.

"Mary Anne and I are old pals," explained Sergeant Johnson. "Colleagues, actually," he added, smiling at me. "How about if I take over from here? I can handle this criminal on my own, I think."

Officer Cleary seemed reluctant to turn me over, but he finally did. Sergeant Johnson

57

asked my father if it was all right if he talked to me privately. "We both know Mary Anne hasn't done anything wrong," he told my dad. "But it's true that she was caught in a compromising situation, and I need to talk to her about what happened."

My father nodded, squeezed my hand, and told me he'd be waiting.

Sergeant Johnson led me to one of the small rooms the police use for questioning people, sat me down, and asked me to tell him exactly what I'd seen and heard in Miller's Park.

I told him the whole story.

He listened carefully, wrote down everything I said, and didn't interrupt once. Then, when I was done, he told me that he believed everything I'd told him. "Except for one thing," he said. "You must have been mistaken about seeing Fowler. We tried to reach him as soon as we heard about the vandalism, but his wife said he's in San Francisco at a convention."

I didn't know what to say. I was pretty positive that the man I'd seen was Fowler, but I didn't want to contradict Sergeant Johnson, not after he'd been so nice to me. I glanced again at the Polaroid pictures he had shown me of the vandalism at the mill. The vandals had broken most of the windows in the place, and also made a mess of things, slapping paint all over. It was strange, I thought, that they hadn't used spray paint. Instead it looked as if the mill had been splashed with house paint. Green house paint.

The next day, the story hit the papers. They couldn't use my name, of course, since I'm a minor, but anyone reading between the lines could have figured out that the YOUTH CAUGHT AT MILL was a member of the BSC, since the article mentioned our protest against Fowler. The article went on to say that no charges had been filed. It also said that the police had discovered that the footprints near the mill were from man-size sneakers, and that the real vandal was still being sought, but I doubted whether everybody read that far. The article also quoted Fowler, who had been reached in San Francisco and asked for a comment. He said something about how ironic it was that "the youth of Stoneybrook would try to destroy what they claim to want to protect."

Kristy was very upset. "This is terrible publicity for the BSC," she wailed.

We all agreed that what had happened was awful — and very suspicious. Had Fowler tried to set me up, in order to ruin the BSC's image and discredit our campaign to save Miller's Park? Even though the article had said that I wasn't a suspect, some people might still believe I'd done something wrong.

I wondered whether Luke, who was in the woods that night and might have seen the whole thing, might hold the key to Fowler's dirty secrets. But Luke, as I already knew, was good at keeping secrets. And, as usual, he wasn't talking. Whoever had warned him not to "tell" had a pretty powerful hold on Luke.

CHAPTER 7

Wednesday

Decisions, decisions. Should this entry go into the BSC notebook? Or the mystery notebook? On the one hand, it has a lot to do with a sitting job. But on the other hand, it has everything to do with the mystery we've become involved in. Yes, a mystery. That's official. And that's why, as the BSC president, I'm making the official decision to go with the mystery notebook. Now, on to the mystery. . . .

Thursday

I'm glad you made the call, Kristy. I wouldn't have known which notebook to write in when we sit for the Martinez kids. I mean, face it. Every single time we sit over there, strange things happen. Like today, for example . . . .

The mystery notebook really had a workout after those two afternoons: Wednesday, when Kristy sat for the Martinezes, and Thursday, when Jessi was their sitter. Both of them wrote up a storm.

What's the mystery notebook? Oops, I forgot to explain that. It's something new. Kristy (naturally) thought it up, after we'd been involved in several mysteries. It seemed to her that we should have one central location for keeping track of clues, suspects, unusual events — all the bits and pieces that you have to try to put together when you're solving a mystery. (We used to write stuff like that down on the backs of envelopes, or math worksheets, or even napkins if we happened to be discussing a case during a meal at Pizza Express.) It's hard to say whether the mystery notebook has made us better detectives, but we're definitely better organized.

Anyway, back to Kristy's and Jessi's experiences at the Martinez house. On Wednesday afternoon, Kristy headed over, feeling a little apprehensive (she told me later) because of what had happened to me the day before. She didn't know what she was going to tell the kids if they asked questions, but she figured they'd be a little upset after seeing their sitter hauled off by the cops.

They weren't.

Or at least, they didn't appear to be. Amalia seemed to have forgotten what had happened. She was her normal, affectionate self. And Luke didn't seem interested in talking about it, even when Kristy brought it up.

"Mary Anne is fine, in case you're wondering," she told them.

Luke nodded. "Cool," he said, looking down at the Power Ranger he was playing with.

"Beary Anne, Peary Anne," Amalia sang happily.

"She wasn't in trouble or anything," Kristy

continued, unsure of how much to say. "The police just wanted to talk to her."

Luke seemed engrossed by his Power Ranger, and Amalia went on singing. Kristy decided that there was no point in talking about it anymore. If they had questions, they could ask her and she'd answer them, but if not it seemed just as well to drop the subject.

"How about a snack?" she asked. "You guys must be hungry." She headed into the kitchen, and both of them followed her. She fixed some peanut butter and jelly on crackers, poured them each a glass of milk, and sat down with them while they ate. By the end of snacktime, Amalia's face, hands, and dress were stained with grape jelly. There was even jelly in her bangs.

"Better clean you up," said Kristy. She turned on the taps in the sink and checked to make sure the water wasn't too hot. Then she picked up Amalia, sat her on the counter, and helped her scrub her hands and face. Just as she was wiping the front of Amalia's dress, the phone rang. Kristy sighed. Her hands were wet and sticky with jelly, and she couldn't leave Amalia sitting on the kitchen counter. "Luke, could you grab that?" she asked. She knows it's best for the sitter to answer the phone, but there are exceptions to every rule.

Luke ran for the phone, which hung on the wall next to the refrigerator. "Hello?" he said. He listened for a second. "Who is this?" he asked. "Hello?" He listened again, and then, suddenly, he hung up the phone with a bang. Kristy turned just in time to see a terrified look on Luke's face.

"What is it?" she asked. "Luke, who was that?"

Luke didn't answer.

"Was somebody saying scary things?" Kristy asked, remembering what I'd told her about the writing on the window.

Luke still didn't answer. He just looked down at his sneakers.

Kristy dabbed one more time at Amalia's dress and then lifted her down. "You sit here and dry off," she said, handing her a paper towel. Then she walked over to the phone, picked up the receiver, and pushed three buttons.

"What are you doing?" asked Luke.

"I'm trying to find out who that was," answered Kristy. "If I dial those three numbers, the phone where that call was made from will ring. Hopefully, someone will pick up, and I can find out who it was that scared you."

Luke didn't look comforted. In fact, he looked more scared than ever, Kristy said later.

Kristy listened while the phone rang. It rang about ten times, and she was just about to give up when somebody answered. A woman. A woman who had been waiting for a bus near a pay phone in downtown Stoneybrook, at the corner of Main and Essex. She told Kristy that she'd just seen a young man using the phone, but that was all she knew.

First there was the phone call. Then there was that episode out in the Martinezes' backyard...

Luke refused to talk about what the caller had said, and finally Kristy just gave up. It was hard enough trying to get through to Luke; she didn't want to annoy him.

Just as Kristy was wiping off the countertop, someone knocked on the door. She ran to answer it, with Amalia in her arms and Luke right behind her. Steig and Benson were at the door. They asked if Luke wanted to come outside with them.

Kristy thought she saw Steig wink at Luke, and Benson seemed to be holding something behind his back, but she didn't think much of it.

66

"Can I go out?" Luke asked her.

"Sure," said Kristy, surprised and pleased. It was the first time Luke had allowed her out of his sight. She made him put on a jacket and, remembering how Luke had run off on me just the day before, told all three boys to stay within shouting distance. Then she looked at Amalia, decided that her dress was still too messy, and took her upstairs to change.

She and Amalia took a while to pick out a clean dress, and then Amalia pleaded with Kristy to read "just one story" from her Peter Rabbit books. Kristy was in the middle of *The Tale of Mrs. Tiggy-Winkle* when she heard a loud whistle, followed by a popping noise. She stopped in mid-sentence to listen, and heard another whistle and pop. "What — " she began, jumping up to run to the window. She saw nothing in the front yard, so she ran to Luke's room to check out the backyard, and was shocked to see the three boys huddled near the swing set, setting off bottle rockets. (Those are little firecrackers attached to a stick; you stand them up in an empty bottle, light them, and they take off into the sky — that's the whistling noise — and explode.)

Kristy grabbed Amalia and thundered down the stairs. She ran out the back door, surprising the boys just as they were about to light one more rocket. "What are you doing?" she demanded as all three boys froze. "Where did you find those matches? Do you know how dangerous that is?" Kristy was beside herself. The boys were silent. Kristy held out a hand, and Steig put the matchbook into it without being asked.

Kristy noticed that his shirt was stained with soot. She knew, from watching her brothers set off bottle rockets, that they don't make much of a mess, so the stain made her wonder. She also remembered that Steig had asked me whether I smoked, and wondered if he had been trying to find a source for matches. Was Steig into fires? Could he have set the one in the Martinezes' garage? Maybe that was Luke's secret. Luke was best friends with Steig, and might be willing to keep silent for him. Then Kristy remembered my telling her that I'd noticed soot on Cary's hands. Was he in on this, too? Had he been the one who wrote "DON'T TELL" on the window? Maybe Fowler wasn't involved after all. Kristy's head was spinning. Something very strange was going on at the Martinez house, and she had the feeling she wasn't going to get to the bottom of it that day. All she could do was send Steig and Benson home and bring Luke back inside for a big lecture on playing with matches and firecrackers.

Kristy, you're absolutely right. Something strange is going on at the Martinezes'. You'll never believe what I found in the yard . . . .

The next day, Jessi sat for Luke and Amalia. She was determined to be friendly to Luke, and hoped he would warm up to her. She didn't have much luck, though. Luke wasn't rude or mean to Jessi, but he was quiet. No matter how hard she tried to involve him in conversation, Luke resisted. And he seemed to stick to her like glue, just as he'd done with the rest of us.

"Is your friend Steig coming over today?" she asked him at one point.

Luke shrugged. "I don't know if he's allowed to play with me for a while," he said. "After yesterday, I think his mom's pretty mad."

That was the closest Luke came to a conversation. Meanwhile, Amalia was climbing all over Jessi, asking about her earrings, about her sweatshirt with a picture of a ballet dancer on it, and about the beads in Jessi's braids.

Eventually, Jessi suggested that they all go out in the backyard for a while. And it was during a game of catch back there that she found the empty tobacco package. "Luke," she said, picking it up. "Do you know who

69

this could belong to?" She tried not to sound accusatory, but she couldn't help wondering if he and the Retlin boys had been lighting up more than rockets.

Luke shrugged, but Jessi thought he looked nervous. "How am I supposed to know?" he asked defensively.

"I thought maybe one of your parents smoked," said Jessi.

"No way," said Luke. And that was the end of it. He wouldn't say another word on the topic, and finally Jessi gave up and stuck the package into her back pocket.

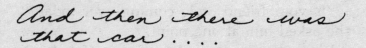

And then there was that car . . . .

Later that afternoon, Jessi was out in the front yard with Luke and Amalia when Steig came over to talk to Luke. "I'm not really supposed to be over here for three days," said Steig. "That's my punishment. But I just came to tell you that."

Luke nodded. "At least it's only three days," he said, punching Steig lightly on the shoulder.

"Hey, look," said Steig. "It's Fowler's car!" He pointed to a black Cadillac that was cruising down the street, away from them.

Jessi thought she saw Luke stiffen. And she

wondered how Steig knew what kind of car Fowler drove.

All in all, the notes from those two days ended up filling a lot of pages in the mystery notebook. But, as Kristy pointed out, even though the phone call, the matches, the tobacco package, and the car were all very interesting and made us suspicious, they weren't what you could call evidence or clues. We were no closer to solving the mystery at the Martinez house, and we weren't any closer to winning our fight with Fowler, either.

CHAPTER 8

"They *what*? Are you trying to tell me you were arrested?"

I held the phone receiver away from my ear and grinned. It's not often I get such a rise out of Dawn. Normally she's so laid-back. "No, I wasn't arrested," I assured her after a second. "They just took me in for questioning, that's all."

"For vandalism?" asked Dawn. "But that's ridiculous. You wouldn't vandalize anything!"

"I know," I said. "But even I have to admit that it looked pretty bad. There I was, standing in the woods, holding a brick in my hand." I started to giggle. "I mean, what was that cop supposed to think?"

"If he knew you, he'd think you were in the wrong place at the wrong time, which you were," said Dawn.

"I guess," I replied. It was great to talk to my stepsister. She'd called that Friday night just to chat, and I'd ended up trying to fill her in on what was going on with Fowler, with Miller's Park, and with our new clients, the Martinezes. I say *trying*, because it wasn't easy. Everything was complicated and messy, full of loose ends and clues that didn't add up.

"So, let me make sure I understand," said Dawn. "This Fowler guy is trying to ruin Miller's Park. Which is, by the way, very bad news. I always loved that place."

She paused for a second, as if she were remembering how the park looked. I felt a twinge of gladness at the idea that she was a little homesick for Connecticut. Maybe if she misses it enough she'll come back someday.

"So the BSC has been trying to fight Fowler with letters to the editor," Dawn continued. "That's great! Do you think it's working?"

"I don't know," I admitted. "I guess we won't know for sure until the town council meeting. That's when everything will be decided, once and for all. And the meeting is, like, less than a week away!"

"Whoa," said Dawn. "That's soon. Okay, we'll go back to that in a second. Now, tell me again about this boy Luke and the fire at his house and all."

I repeated everything that had happened at the Martinezes'. The fire, the bottle rocket episode, Luke's odd behavior — including his fear of Fowler's car; everything.

"So," said Dawn, when I'd finished. "It sounds to me like what's going on with the Martinezes might be related to Fowler. I don't know how, but I bet it is. After all, he has a real motive for forcing them to move away. And I think Luke may know something, but it sounds like you can't press him for information. Somebody else may be intimidating him, and you don't want to add to that."

I couldn't argue with her. For one thing, Dawn's a good detective. For another, she was giving me an objective viewpoint, which is always helpful. Also, Kristy had said some of the same things. And finally, the fact was that I agreed with her. I believed that, somehow, Fowler was mixed up in the strange happenings at the Martinez house. He might even be responsible for the fire. As Dawn said, he had the motive. I just didn't know how to prove it, and that made me angry. I hated to think of poor Luke feeling so threatened.

"Okay," said Dawn, "back to that meeting. It seems to me that what you have to do is find some real dirt on Fowler, something that will prove to the town council that he shouldn't be allowed to develop Miller's Park."

"You're right," I said. "And we have to act

74

fast, too. There isn't much time left." If we were going to stop Fowler, my friends and I had to work fast. I said a hurried "Thanks-so-much! Miss-you! Bye!" to Dawn, hung up, and immediately called Kristy.

"How about meeting me at the library first thing tomorrow?" I asked, before she'd even finished saying "hello." "I think we have some work to do. Oh, and can you call some of the others?" I explained what I wanted to do.

Kristy seemed a bit surprised at the way I'd taken charge, but she didn't hesitate. "I'll call Abby, Shannon, Jessi, and Mal," she said. "You call Claudia and Stacey — and see if Logan wants to come, too. The more the merrier."

Good thing the Stoneybrook Public Library is open — and not too crowded — on Saturday mornings. We met on the front steps at about nine-thirty. Kristy made it, and Claudia (who was yawning and eating a jelly dough-nut) and Stacey were both there. Mal and Jessi were sitting for Mal's brothers and sisters, and Shannon was helping with a French club car wash, but Logan had come, and so had Abby.

"So what's the deal?" asked Logan, stretch-ing. He looked sleepy and kind of cute, like a little boy who just woke up. His hair was stick-ing up in the back, as if he'd forgotten to comb it. "What are we here for?"

"To find out whatever we can about Reginald Fowler," I announced. "Hopefully that'll include some dirt we can report to the press, to the Historical Society, and to the members of the town council."

"Anyone for a doughnut?" asked Claudia, passing around a bag. "They'll help us think better."

"In that case, I'll have two," said Abby, reaching into the bag. "I'm not used to thinking at all this early on a Saturday morning."

The rest of us helped ourselves, too, except for Stacey, who had brought a banana.

A few minutes later, we headed into the library's reference room. We've worked there many times before, and not always on school projects. The library is a really good place to start when you're investigating a mystery, and we've found important clues there more than once. At first, we weren't sure where to begin, but Claudia's mother, who is the head librarian, helped us out. Now we're pros with the microfilm, the periodical indexes, and the card catalog.

We started right in on the *Stoneybrook News*, using two microfilm machines to cruise through as many past issues as we could. We scanned the indexes, looking for Reginald Fowler's name. Logan and I, working together, were the first ones to hit paydirt.

"Check it out!" said Logan, flipping to an article from a couple of years back. We read it, and then another related article from a week later, and then another.

All of them were about a development project Fowler had tried to push through in the nearby town of Lawrenceville. Apparently, he had wanted to build a "townhouse community" that would include a mall, a huge superstore, and a gym, as well as a bunch of condos. The hitch? The tract of land he had picked out was what some people in the community thought of as an "unspoiled area" that ought to stay that way.

The war was on. As we read through the articles one by one, the story unfolded. First, Fowler tried to convince Lawrenceville that the development was in the town's best interests. Then the people who were opposing him brought in environmental specialists. Fowler brought in other specialists, who debated them. The townspeople held a huge rally. Fowler rounded up some "friends" who staged a counter-rally for the TV news. Finally, the townspeople proved that the land could be classified as a wetland and therefore as a protected area. At the same time, Fowler was accused of bribing town officials. Soon after, the charges were dropped and he disappeared, never to be heard from again.

"All *right!*" I cried, as I read the last article. Logan held up his hand, and I gave him a high five.

"Shhh!" said Kristy, from the other side of the table, where she and Claudia were working at another microfilm machine.

"Oops," I said, blushing. I'd forgotten where I was. Reading those articles had been like watching a suspense movie. I was on the edge of my seat, and I was thrilled when the good guys won. "Sorry," I told Kristy. "It's just that — "

"Hold on," she said, waving a hand at me. "We're trying to concentrate here. There's something funny going on."

"What is it?" I asked. I leaned forward. "More bribery accusations?"

"No, his record seems clear here in Stoneybrook. It's just that Fowler's birthplace seems to vary in every article we've read about him," she said. "I mean, in one interview he says he was born in Boston — "

" — and in another they quote him as saying he was born in Winnetka, wherever that is," Claudia added.

"So?" I asked. "Maybe somebody just made a mistake."

Kristy shook her head. "No, there's something fishy about it," she said. "His birthdate is always the same: January second. But the place keeps changing."

"Look, here's another one!" said Claudia just then, pointing to the screen. "Here he says he was born in Seattle!"

Abby and Stacey, who had been looking through some books of Stoneybrook history, joined us. "What's going on?" asked Stacey.

Kristy and Claudia explained.

"What if you go back to the earliest mention you can find of him?" asked Abby.

Kristy held up a finger as she flipped through the indexes. "Okay, here it is," she said. "Whoa! This one says he was born in Stoneybrooke, England."

"How totally weird," Stacey commented. "Maybe he's not even a U.S. citizen."

"No, he definitely is," said Kristy. "He makes a point of saying so in every article."

"So — so maybe he was actually born in Stoneybrook, *Connecticut*," I said. "How do we find out?"

Logan snapped his fingers. "Hospital records," he replied. "We used them once for a research project in social studies. They list all the births, going way back."

We made it over to the hospital in no time. On the way, Abby and Stacey told us they'd found something interesting in an old book about Stoneybrook. "Miller's Park used to be called Carter Park," said Abby. "Remember how Fowler called it that? I wonder if that means anything."

"It must," I said. "I bet anything it means he spent time around here in the past."

Guess what? I was right. At least, I'm pretty sure I was. Here's what we found out at the hospital when we looked at the records for the year Reginald Fowler was born: There were five babies born in Stoneybrook on January second of that year. Three of them were girls. The other two were boys — *twin* boys. Identical twins named John and Samuel Wolfer.

Wolfer.

Fowler.

Same letters, different arrangement.

Coincidence? I didn't think so.

CHAPTER 9

Monday

Okay, once again
I'm writing up a
baby-sitting job
in the mystery note-
book. Why? Guess.
Because I was
sitting for the Martin-
ezes, of course. And
there's always some-
thing mysterious
going on over there.

It was Abby's first time at the Martinezes'. She'd wanted to wait until the smoke smell had cleared away a little more, because of her allergies. And although she could still detect a lingering smoky odor in the house, it wasn't enough to make her sneezy. But Abby wasn't happy.

She'd heard all about Luke from the rest of us, and she knew that we'd each tried our best to reach out to him, and that we'd each felt like total failures. She was determined to be the one to break down his defenses and find out what was bothering him. And, if she could do that, she was sure she could also find out what it was he knew and wasn't telling. But first, she had to win his confidence.

Abby had come prepared. She and the kids were sitting out on the front steps soon after she'd arrived, when she pulled something out of her backpack. "How about some cookies, kids?" she asked, showing them a container she'd brought. "My sister and I made these last night, and I thought you'd like some." (Of course, Abby had checked with Mrs. Martinez to make sure it was okay to give the kids cookies for their afternoon snack.)

Amalia's eyes grew round when she looked into the container. "M-Ms!" she said happily.

Abby laughed. "That's right, they have

M&Ms on them," she said. "Go ahead, take a couple."

Amalia reached in with both hands and came up with a cookie in each. She grinned at Abby. "I love cookies," she said in a gruff voice. "Me Cookie Monster!"

Abby cracked up and reached out to hug Amalia, who hugged her back. Then Abby offered the cookies to Luke. He eyed them suspiciously. "I'm not hungry," he said.

"Not hungry?" Abby asked. "What does that have to do with cookies? Cookies are just for fun, whether you're hungry or not!" She smiled at Luke, but he didn't smile back. He did, however, reach in and pull out one cookie. Then he moved away from where Abby was sitting and nibbled on it thoughtfully, examining it now and then as if he thought it might be poisoned.

Abby watched him and rolled her eyes. This was going to be harder than she thought. She saw him finish his cookie and held out the container. "Another, Luke? Aren't they great? My mom's famous secret recipe."

Luke, who had reluctantly agreed to another cookie, seemed to jump a bit when Abby said the word "secret." She pretended not to notice.

In the end, Luke ate four cookies and Amalia had three. Abby was pleased, even though

Luke still wasn't exactly acting friendly. She figured it was a start.

She bent to put the container away.

"Well, hey there, kiddies!" she heard. She looked up to see a pipe-smoking man approaching.

"Who's that?" she whispered to Luke.

"Mr. Fontecchio," he whispered back.

Abby nodded. She remembered reading about a pipe-smoking neighbor in the mystery notebook. "Hi," she said. "I'm Abby, the baby-sitter."

"And I'm Mr. Fontecchio, the neighbor," the man replied, with a fake-sounding chuckle. "Just checking up on things," he added. "I, uh, promised Mr. Martinez I'd keep an eye out, you know."

"For what?" asked Luke.

"Oh, you know," said Mr. Fontecchio, looking a little nervous. He took his pipe out of his mouth, examined it, and stuck it back in. "My brothers and I care about our neighborhood, that's all."

"Sure you do," said Luke, not even trying to hide a sneer. "That's why you're selling to — to that guy Fowler."

"Luke!" said Abby, surprised at how rude he was being. "Sorry," she said to Mr. Fontecchio.

He waved a hand. "No problem," he said.

"No problem at all." Then he wandered off.

"Why doesn't he just go back to his house?" hissed Luke.

"Isn't that what he's doing?" asked Abby.

"No, he lives over there," Luke said, pointing to the house to the right of the Martinezes'.

"Hmmm," said Abby. It was true that Mr. Fontecchio seemed to be walking away from his house. And, as he walked, he appeared to be examining and inspecting everything he saw: every flower, every brick in the path, every tree. Abby thought his behavior was suspicious. "Does he always act — strange?" she asked Luke.

Luke shook his head. "No — I don't know," he said, reverting to his usual unapproachable attitude.

Abby thought about the fact that Mr. Fontecchio was smoking a pipe, and she wondered if he was the one who had left the empty tobacco package in the Martinezes' backyard. Then she thought about why it was that Luke had run across the street to the Retlins', rather than next door to the Fontecchios', when the fire had broken out. After all, the Fontecchios' was closer. Was there something about Mr. Fontecchio that frightened Luke? Or was it just that Luke didn't like the man? Next, Abby thought about the settlement Mr. Fontecchio and his brothers were due to receive from

Fowler. She realized that if the Martinezes held out and refused to sell, the whole development could be jeopardized — and the Fontecchios would never see their money. Were they the ones behind the fire? They certainly had a motive.

"Abby!"

Abby jumped. "What is it?" she asked Amalia, her heart beating fast. Amalia had practically yelled into her ear.

"I want a drink."

"Oh, okay," said Abby. "Let's go inside and see what there is." She took a deep breath, trying to calm herself. Maybe it would be better to save the detective work for later. "How about you, Luke? Ready for a drink?"

"I guess," said Luke.

They all headed inside, and Abby poured three glasses of grape juice. They sat down around the table. "I know!" said Abby. "I heard about a new game today. Want to try it?"

"What is it?" asked Amalia eagerly.

"It's called 'Secrets,' " explained Abby. She was winging it, she told me later, making up the game on the spot. It was really just another ploy to draw out Luke. "What you do is, um, you have to tell the person next to you a secret, something you've never told anybody else before."

Amalia's face lit up. "Fun!"

Luke looked suspicious, so Abby decided to put him at ease. "I'll start by telling Luke something," she said. "Then you can tell Amalia something," she continued. "Okay?"

"Fine," said Luke.

Abby leaned over and whispered in his ear. "Once I let my sister be punished for something I did," she said.

Luke looked at her. "Really?" he asked.

"Really," she said. "Now you tell Amalia something."

She pretended not to listen, but she thought she overheard something about "chocolate bunny," and she smiled to herself. Luke was confessing some childhood crime.

Amalia giggled. "Now I tell you something," she said to Abby. She leaned over and whispered wetly into Abby's ear, "I love Barney."

Abby tried to hide her smile. "Okay," she said, hoping she'd succeeded in putting Luke at ease, by having him tell Amalia a secret first. "Now let's turn it the other way. I'll tell Amalia something, and we'll go around that way." She bent down to Amalia's ear. "I love the tooth fairy," she whispered.

Amalia giggled some more. Then she turned and whispered in Luke's ear. This time, Abby overheard something about "Mommy." Amalia was loving the game.

"Okay, Luke, now you tell me something," said Abby. "Remember, it should be something you've never told anybody. Something you've been keeping secret."

Luke looked at her. Then, suddenly, he pushed his chair back. "This is a dumb game," he announced, standing up and grabbing his empty glass. He put it into the sink. "I'm not playing anymore."

Abby sighed. She'd been so close! She had a feeling that Luke really wanted to let go of his secret, but couldn't. "Come on, Luke," she said teasingly. "You can trust me."

Luke met her eyes, just for a second. Then he dropped his gaze to his feet. "But you're a *baby-sitter!*"

"I — " Abby began, confused by his response. Just then the phone rang. "I'll answer it!" she said. She took the call, which was for Mrs. Martinez, and wrote down a message. By the time she'd hung up, Luke and Amalia had moved into the living room. Luke had plugged in a video game — he was allowed to play for half an hour a day — and Amalia was pulling out her paper doll collection. Abby decided to let matters drop. She'd tried hard, but Luke was no nearer to opening up with her than he'd been with any of the other BSC members.

Abby began to tidy up the room, piling books and magazines on a coffee table and tossing toys into a chest in the corner. Luke's game beeped and buzzed, filling the room with sound. Amalia sang to her dolls.

Abby bent down to pull one more book out from under the couch. "Here's your notebook, Luke," she said.

He glanced around. "Not mine," he answered. Then he went back to his game.

"Allie!" said Amalia.

Abby looked up, figuring that Amalia was talking to one of her dolls. But she was looking at the notebook Abby held. "What?" asked Abby.

"Nothing," said Luke, turning again to glare at Amalia. "She's mixed up."

Abby shrugged and took a closer look at the notebook. Of course it wasn't Luke's. She should have known that right away. On the front it said *Stoneybrook Day School*, and Abby knew very well that Luke went to Stoneybrook Elementary. Besides, the lines were too narrow for a kid his age. Abby flipped through the pages, but there were no notes. Just one page covered with hearts, with the initials "B.R." inside them.

"Hmmm," said Abby, flipping it shut. It was just a notebook, but she had a feeling it might also be some kind of clue. She decided to bring it up at that afternoon's BSC meeting.

CHAPTER 10

"Any other business?" Kristy asked at our meeting that afternoon. We were all gathered in Claudia's room, including Abby, who had just finished her job at the Martinezes'. Stacey had already collected our dues, since it was a Monday, and Claudia had already dug a bag of marshmallows out of her closet and passed them around. (Stacey was ignoring the marshmallows and munching away on some pretzels instead.)

"Well, I'd like to report that Luke completely opened up to me today," began Abby. We didn't let her continue. We were all too excited. Everybody started to talk at once.

"You're kidding!" cried Mal.

"He *did?*" asked Jessi.

"That's, like, totally excellent!" exclaimed Claudia.

"Awesome!" said Stacey.

"How did you do it?" asked Kristy.

"What exactly did he tell you?" I asked.

"Whoa, whoa, slow down, guys," said Abby with a giggle. "I didn't say that Luke *did* open up to me. I just said I'd like to report that he did. But I can't — because he didn't. He acted the same way he always has, and I didn't find out a thing."

Suddenly, the room was a lot quieter.

"Oh," said Kristy finally.

The rest of us were silent. I, for one, was really disappointed, but also, in a way, just a little bit glad. I think I'd secretly hoped that if Luke ever did open up, it would be to me. After all, I'm the one who's known for being sensitive and a good listener. I was still hoping I could somehow draw him out, help him climb out of that shell he seemed to be trapped in.

"It's so frustrating!" said Stacey, echoing my thoughts. "I mean, something really fishy is going on, and it looks more and more as if it's all connected — the fire, Fowler, everything. It would be great if we could convince Luke to talk, but we can't. So what do we do?"

"I think we should try to find out more about that fire at the Martinezes' on our own," said Kristy, smacking her fist into her hand. "Since we can't seem to find out the truth from Luke, we'll have to find it ourselves."

"You know, you're right," said Stacey. "I'm sitting over there tomorrow. Maybe I can do some investigating then."

"I'll come over, too," said Kristy. "As long as it's okay with the Martinezes. I'll call them later and ask."

"If they say yes, I'll go, too," I said. "Maybe we can find some clues if we look hard enough. But you know, I don't think checking out that fire is enough. I think we also have to keep trying to find out more about Fowler," I continued, remembering what Dawn had said. "We need ammunition for that town council meeting, especially if we can't prove he's responsible for the fire."

"I'm sure the people at the Historical Society would love it if we could dig up some dirt on Fowler," said Stacey. "I heard that they're putting together a report for the meeting, about how important Ambrose's Sawmill is as a historical asset to the town. But I have a feeling that won't be enough to convince the town council."

Claudia leaned back on her bed and sighed. "So in other words, we're all back to square one."

"Well, not totally," said Abby. "I mean, we did find out about those Wolfer twins who were born on the same date as Fowler. That seems like a lead to me."

"Maybe it is," said Mal. "But what do we do about it?"

"Find out more," replied Jessi, speaking into the floor. She was doing one of her ballet stretches, the kind that always looks (to me) as if it would be incredibly painful. Her legs were stretched out wide, and she'd bent her whole upper body down so that her nose was nearly touching the floor.

"More about what?" I asked.

Jessi straightened up. "I don't know," she admitted. "More about the twins? Maybe if Fowler really does have a twin brother we should locate him. He might be able to give us some information."

"Or maybe the twin is the one who's been up to no good," said Stacey slowly. She sounded as if she were working something out as she spoke. "Remember the night you were arrested?" she asked, turning to me.

I nodded. How could I forget?

"Well, when you told Sergeant Johnson you saw Fowler out by the old sawmill, he said you couldn't have — "

" — because Fowler was in San Francisco!" I finished, excited. "And you're saying that maybe the person I saw was Fowler's twin!"

Stacey grinned and nodded.

"Whoa!" said Claudia. "Now *that's* an interesting idea." She leaned forward, and her eyes were sparkling. "It sounds like something out of a Nancy Drew book. 'The Case of the Treacherous Twins!' I can see it now."

"I'm confused. You're saying that we're actually dealing with Reginald Fowler's evil twin brother?" asked Abby.

"They're *both* evil," I said. "I mean, we know Fowler has no respect or caring for Stoneybrook. So he's no good guy. But maybe his twin does some of his dirty work." I nodded. This was really an interesting idea.

"So we have to track down the twin," said Mal.

"Both twins, actually," I said. "We don't really know which one is which. So we need to find out everything we can about both — " I grabbed the mystery notebook and flipped to the right page "— John and Samuel Wolfer."

Just then, the phone rang, and I think we all jumped a little. I'd almost forgotten we were in the middle of a club meeting, and I think the others felt the same way.

Kristy answered the phone and we snapped back into BSC mode. It was Mrs. Braddock, one of our regular clients. I checked the record book to figure out who could take the job. Claudia and Jessi were the only ones free. Jessi said she had a special ballet class that day, so Claudia ended up with the job. Kristy called

Mrs. Braddock back, and as soon as she hung up, the phone rang again. From then on, the meeting was a busy one, and we didn't have another chance to talk about what to do next.

At six, when the meeting was officially over, we all stayed an extra five minutes in order to make a plan. We agreed that Kristy, Stacey, and I would do some detective work at the Martinezes' the next afternoon. Also, we'd try to come up with some ideas for investigating the Wolfer twins.

It was a pretty loose plan, but after dinner that night, when I started to think about it, I came up with an idea. What about that development project we'd read about, the one in Lawrenceville? Why had they chosen that town? Maybe, I thought, because one or both of the Wolfer twins lived there!

How could I find out if I was right? I knew we didn't have a Lawrenceville phone book in the house, and it was too late to go to the library. On an impulse, I dialed directory assistance.

"What city, please?" asked the operator.

"Lawrenceville," I answered, glad that my dad and Sharon had gone out and couldn't overhear what I was doing and ask questions. It wouldn't be easy to explain.

"Name?" asked the operator.

"Wolfer," I said. "W-O-L-F-E-R. Samuel Wolfer."

"I have no listing under that name," she reported.

"Thank you," I said. I hung up, disappointed. What a dead end. Then I shook myself. I'd forgotten to ask about *John* Wolfer. I dialed again — and, just in case I reached the same operator, I disguised my voice by pinching my nose.

"What city, please?"

"Lawrenceville," I replied, sounding as if I had the worst cold in the world.

"Name?" she asked.

I couldn't tell if it was the same operator or not, so I kept pinching my nose. "Wolfer," I told her. I spelled it out again. "John Wolfer."

"No listing," said the operator. Did she sound suspicious, or was it just my imagination?

"Thanks," I said, hanging up. Bummer. That hadn't worked either. I sat and thought for a second, and then jumped up and ran for a pencil and some paper. I sat down again and made a list of possible names, ones that were close to Wolfer. Then I made a few more calls, working my way from Wolfman, Samuel to Wolfstein, John. For each call, I put on a different accent. I was starting to crack myself up.

Finally, one call (I was using a French accent) hit paydirt. "Why, yes," the operator said. "I do have a listing for a Samuel Wolf in Lawrenceville. The number is — "

I barely listened. After all, I didn't really need his phone number. All I needed to know was that he existed, and that he lived in Lawrenceville. Was Samuel Wolf really our man? In order to know for sure, I'd have to find out his birthdate. How could I do that?

I looked around the living room, glancing at the bookcases that line one wall. Then my eye lit on a burgundy-colored book shelved next to my dad's law texts. "Perfect!" I said to myself, recognizing it. I pulled it out. *Who's Who in Southern Connecticut*," I said out loud, reading the title. My dad had shown me where his name was in that book, and once when Kristy and I were browsing through it we'd also found an entry for Watson Brewer. Just about anyone who was involved in politics, law, or business in our area is in that book. I sat down with it, crossed my fingers, and turned straight to the Ws. Then, suddenly, it popped out at me: "Wolf, Samuel." Just what I was looking for! Or was it? Quickly, I read the beginning of the entry. "Born January 2nd . . ." It was him! It had to be.

I read on. The short biography didn't reveal much about the man, but it did mention that he was a twin, and it gave the basic information about his childhood and his parents. Both were dead: The mother died one day after the twins were born — how tragic — and the father died (I quickly did the math) when they were seven.

The most interesting thing I found was that the "childhood home" of Samuel Wolf was a "small, rustic cabin." And, believe it or not, that cabin was in Stoneybrook, Connecticut — on a little lane that is now part of Miller's Park!

It meant something. I knew it did. But *what?*

CHAPTER 11

Tuesday

Here we go again with a baby-sitting job that has to be written up in the mystery notebook. We're really filling these pages up fast! Soon we'll need a whole notebook just for notes on "Weird Things That Happen at the Martinezes'...."

The events Stacey recorded in the mystery notebook sounded pretty strange, and they would have sounded even stranger if I hadn't been there myself to see what had happened.

As we'd planned, Kristy and I showed up at the Martinezes' on Tuesday, not long after Stacey arrived. It turned out that Mr. Martinez had come home that afternoon. He still needed a sitter, though, since his plan was to spend a few hours grading a pile of papers. He didn't mind if Kristy and I came over, as long as we kept the kids occupied so he could work in peace. He was more than happy to hear that our plans included a garage clean-up.

Luke did not seem at all thrilled to have three baby-sitters on hand, but Amalia was in heaven. "Staceee! Kisty! May Anne!" she crowed, hugging each of us in turn.

Stacey had already explained to Luke that we'd planned to work on cleaning up the garage (that was our cover story for the investigating we wanted to do) and that we'd need his help. He wasn't overjoyed, but he agreed, probably because he didn't want to let us out of his sight. Amalia didn't seem to care what we did, as long as one of us carried her around piggyback style.

We headed into the garage, and Stacey showed Luke a pile of old magazines that needed sorting. Some of them had been damaged by the fire, but some of them were salvageable. Mr. and Mrs. Martinez wanted to save the good ones for use in their classrooms. Luke seemed happy to have a job to do, and he took the magazines out into the driveway where he could sit while he sorted. Although the big roll-up garage door was closed, the regular-size door next to it was open, and he kept an eye on us through that.

Once he was settled in, the three of us began to prowl around the garage, looking for clues. I wasn't sure exactly what I was searching for. It wasn't as if the person who started the fire would have dropped a business card or anything. But maybe, even if we couldn't figure out who had started the fire, we could find out more about the fire itself.

"Like, maybe there are some matches lying around, or a lighter," Kristy had said, as she and I were riding bikes (she'd borrowed Dawn's, which is still stored in our barn) to the Martinezes' that day. "If we can figure out how the fire was started in the first place, that might lead us to other clues."

The Martinezes' garage was very neat, so it didn't take long for us to realize that there were no matches lying around. There weren't any gasoline cans, either, or any other clues as to how the fire had started. I was disappointed.

"We'll never figure this out," I said quietly, so Amalia wouldn't hear. "There isn't a clue in sight. Maybe this was a totally innocent fire. Maybe it has nothing to do with Fowler."

"Maybe," said Kristy doubtfully. "But I bet it does. Don't forget that he has a big motive."

Stacey, who was carrying Amalia on her back, gave her a little boost to put her in a better position. Amalia giggled. "Uppy, uppy," she sang happily, laughing and leaning her head back so she was staring at the ceiling while Stacey jounced her.

The three of us laughed, too. Amalia's giggle was contagious. For a second, I forgot how frustrated I was by this mystery. I leaned my head back, too, just to make Amalia laugh again. "Uppy, uppy," I said, copying her. It worked. She laughed some more, so I kept it up. "Uppy — whoa!" I said, staring harder at the ceiling. "Hey, guys. Check it out!" I pointed to the ceiling. They followed my gaze.

"So?" Kristy said, after she'd taken a look.

"See the sooty streaks?" I asked.

"Sure," said Stacey. "They're from the fire."

"Right," I said. "But Mrs. Martinez told me that the garage door was *open* at the time of the fire."

Kristy was looking at me closely. "Uh-huh," she said. "What are you saying, Mary Anne?"

I was excited. "Look at the garage door now," I said. "It's closed, right?"

Stacey and Kristy looked at me as if I were speaking another language. "Well, duh," remarked Stacey. "But so what?"

I walked to the garage door, bent over, and yanked on the handle. The door rolled up to reveal Luke, who was sitting cross-legged on the driveway, sorting magazines. I waved at Luke and turned to my friends. "If the door had been open," I explained, "there wouldn't be any soot on the ceiling. See?" I pointed to the ceiling, which was now covered by the rolled-up door.

"Whoa!" exclaimed Kristy.

"That changes a lot," said Stacey. "That means that the door must have been opened *after* the fire started. So — so whoever started the fire must have been in here, with the door closed."

"Not only that," said Kristy suddenly. "I think they may have tried to put out the fire, too." She had been rummaging through a pile of rags, and she held something up. It was a fire extinguisher. "I can't believe I just found this now," she said, looking it over more closely. "And check it out, the gauge says 'empty.' Somebody used this up."

We all looked at each other. "Well," I said, "this tells us something. I don't know what, but it's *something*." I tried to sound enthusiastic, but in reality I was feeling discouraged. Even though we'd discovered some new clues, we were really no closer to figuring out who had started the fire.

"I'm done!" Luke declared just then, as he carried two piles of magazines back into the garage. He dumped one pile into the trash can and put the other one on a shelf. "Can we do something else now?"

Kristy, Stacey, and I exchanged looks. I shrugged. So did Kristy.

"Sure," said Stacey. "Let's go for a walk." I knew she wanted to keep the kids out of the house, where their dad was trying to work.

"Okay," agreed Luke.

"Yea!" shouted Amalia, bouncing up and down on Stacey's back.

"Want me to take Amalia for a little bit?" I offered.

"Sure," said Stacey. Kristy and Luke walked ahead while we stopped to make the trade.

After a minute, we caught up. Amalia was encouraging me to trot by kicking her heels into my sides and calling, "Go, horsie, go!"

"Nice horse, Amalia!" I heard someone call.

I looked across the street and saw Cary Retlin and his brothers playing catch in their yard. I stuck out my tongue at him.

"Can we go over and play with them?" asked Luke.

Stacey hesitated.

"Why don't you go on over by yourself, Luke?" suggested Kristy. "We'll be along in a few minutes."

Now Luke hesitated. As usual, he didn't seem to want to be far from his sitter — or sitters, in this case.

"Go ahead," I urged him. I could tell that he was torn.

"Okay," he said. "See you later." After checking for cars he crossed the street.

"Great. This gives us time to poke around the area some more," said Kristy.

"Poke!" squealed Amalia, poking me in the shoulder. "Come on, Pokey!" She kicked her heels into me again, and I started to trot along.

"Who lives here?" asked Kristy, pointing to the house we were walking by. "Is that Mr. Fontecchio's house?"

I shook my head. "No, he's the next-door neighbor on the other side," I told her. "I don't know whose house this is."

All of a sudden, Stacey stopped in midstep. "Well, whoever they are, I think they're about to have a flooded basement," she said. She pointed to a basement window on the side of the house. It was broken, and a hose, which came from the back of the house, was hanging down into the cellar.

"Oh, no!" I cried. I checked the driveway and saw that it was empty; nobody seemed to be home. Meanwhile, Kristy ran over to take a closer look. She pulled out the hose, and, sure enough, it was running. "I'll turn it off," she called. She tore off around the side of the house to find the tap.

Stacey had run to the door of the house and was knocking on it, but nobody answered.

"Let's go tell Mr. Martinez," I said.

That did not turn out to be the greatest idea. Why? Well, because Mr. Martinez, who happened to know that his neighbors were away for two weeks, decided he'd better call the police. And the police were suspicious — of us! It took Mr. Martinez ten minutes to convince the officer he was speaking to that we had been busy watching his children, and that we had had nothing to do with the vandalism.

Once again, I had managed to be in the wrong place at the wrong time.

"I wonder if somebody's trying to frame us," Kristy mused as we headed back outside a few minutes later. Now she was carrying Amalia, who was thrilled to have three "horsies" so that she never had to walk.

"Mr. Martinez sure was nice about it," commented Stacey.

I agreed. After he'd hung up, I'd apologized and told him we'd understand if he didn't want us to baby-sit for his kids anymore. After all, who wants sitters who are always under suspicion? But he had insisted that he was very happy with the BSC — to Kristy's obvious relief.

Then we'd had a very interesting conversation about the Martinezes' old baby-sitter. I asked why she'd left, and he told us that he didn't know. "Maybe Allie was scared by the fire," he'd said. "She quit right after that."

Allie! That was the name Amalia had called me. Maybe she was the owner of that Stoneybrook Day School notebook Abby had found. Maybe we needed to find out more about this Allie person.

"Without notice?" Kristy asked Mr. Martinez, interrupting my thoughts. He nodded.

Kristy couldn't believe that, and she said so as we walked over to the Retlins' to collect Luke. "I can't imagine abandoning a client with no notice, just because of a little fire."

"Maybe there's more to it than that," said Stacey.

"Maybe this has something to do with why Luke doesn't trust baby-sitters," I suggested.

"I think we should find this Allie and talk to her."

We had reached the Retlins' yard, As I watched Cary play catch with the younger boys, I suddenly remembered the soot on his shirt. This seemed as good a time as any to confront him about it. I decided that the direct approach was best, so I took a deep breath and walked right over to where he was standing. "You know, Cary," I began, "I'm curious about why I've seen you — and your brother — with soot on your clothes. You didn't have anything to do with that fire at the Martinezes', did you?"

He just looked at me and laughed. "You'd better brush up on your detective skills, Mary Anne." He pointed to a ladder propped against his house. "We've been helping my dad clean the chimney, that's all."

I nodded. I just don't trust Cary Retlin, and I didn't believe a word he was telling me.

"You don't believe me, do you?" he said, as if he were reading my mind. "Well, here's a little tip. Check under Luke's bed. According to Steig, there's something important there."

"Okay, Cary," I said tiredly. "Sure." I knew he was just trying to send me on one of his wild-goose chases. He's done it before when he knew the BSC was involved in a mystery.

He'd probably planted a mouse trap under the bed or something. I just shook my head and walked away.

Mysterious clues. Frame-ups. No real suspects. And time was running out. Solving this mystery was hard enough, without Cary's "help."

CHAPTER 12

"Can you believe it?" asked Kristy, smacking the back of her hand against the newspaper. She'd spotted the article at breakfast that morning and had brought the family's copy to school to show the rest of us. "We had absolutely nothing to do with this — we may have even saved that house from being flooded — and what happens? More bad publicity!"

It was lunchtime on Wednesday, and Kristy was completely ignoring her "Fish Sand. on Bun w/Coleslaw," as that day's menu put it. Instead, she was ranting and raving about how our experience the day before had made it into the paper.

"Don't worry, Kristy," I said, squeezing some tartar sauce out of a little pouch onto my Fish Sand. "It's just the police blotter. They have to report every call they receive. It's only two tiny lines, and it doesn't even mention any names. Plus it explains that we had an alibi."

"Meanwhile, here's something else interesting," said Abby, who had grabbed another section of the paper. "It sounds as if Fowler has a good alibi, too; he's out in California again. He's quoted as saying that he'll definitely be back for tomorrow's town council meeting, though."

Kristy groaned. "I can't believe that meeting is tomorrow night," she said. "We have just over twenty-four hours to crack this case and prove that Fowler is up to no good."

I frowned. "I just *know* that was him out by the mill that night. Unless — unless it was his twin brother! Either way, he *must* be connected with the vandalism. If only we could prove it!"

"I still think he may have been connected with the fire at the Martinezes', too," added Claudia. "Which means he also may be the one threatening Luke to keep quiet."

"Oooh, that man!" I said. It made me so mad to think of anyone threatening a little kid.

Kristy sat up in her seat. "I know!" she said. "Thinking about those threats reminds me. What if we stake out that phone booth at the corner of Essex and Main, the one the call came from that day I was sitting for Luke? Maybe we'll find something out."

112

It seemed like a long shot, but I agreed to check it out, if Logan would come with me.

We talked a bit more at lunch that day about all the possible leads we could follow up (including keeping an eye on Cary Retlin, who was hanging around near our table looking suspicious), and by the time we threw out the remains of our Fish Sand.s, we had a plan. Kristy and Abby had agreed to find Shannon after school and see if she could bring to the BSC meeting a Stoneybrook Day School yearbook that might feature Allie, the Martinezes' previous sitter. Claudia, who was sitting for the Martinezes that afternoon, agreed to keep a close eye out for clues. And Stacey said she'd head back to the library to try to find out more about Fowler. We'd check with Jessi and Mal later (they eat lunch at a different time) to see what they wanted to do. There wasn't much time left. We needed to mobilize the whole BSC detective team.

As it turned out, Jessi joined Stacey at the library, while Mal came with Logan and me to stake out the phone booth. The three of us met right after school and headed downtown. Logan suggested stopping for a bite to eat at the Rosebud Cafe (he's *always* hungry), but I didn't want to take the time. "Maybe later," I said. "First let's check things out." I glanced at my watch. I couldn't stop thinking about how soon the town council meeting would take place. The future of Miller's Park was at stake. We had to do everything we could to save it and put Fowler out of business once and for all. Any so-called businessman who would stoop to threatening a kid deserved to be put in jail.

When we arrived at the corner of Essex and Main, Mal spotted a bench at a nearby bus stop, within sight of the phone booth. "Let's sit here," she suggested. "We can watch all the action."

Ten minutes later, we realized that "action" wasn't exactly the word. I mean, the corner of Essex and Main is a fairly busy one, but there still wasn't much going on. And nobody was using the phone booth. It just stood there, empty. Once in a while somebody walked by it, but nobody stopped to make a call.

Mal and Logan and I sat together quietly, waiting to see if anything would happen. After a while, I noticed Logan yawning. I had to admit that what we were doing was pretty boring, but stakeouts always are. You wait and wait, and sometimes nothing happens.

To distract myself, I started to look around at all the stores on the block. On one side of Essex I saw Pierre's Dry Cleaners, Zuzu's Petals (a flower store with lots of tulips in the window), and Greetings, which looked like a new card shop. On the other side were Sew Fine, a sewing store I shop at sometimes, Baby and Company, a children's clothing store, and the pet store, which is called Fur 'n' Feathers (I buy toys for Tigger there once in a while). On Main, the stores are less interesting: a drugstore, two banks, a coffee shop, and a hardware store. None of the Main Street shops have pretty window displays or cute names, unless you count the pyramid of paint cans in the window of Ted's Tools, which is the name of the hardware store that sits on the corner near the phone booth.

I remembered that Claudia had once gone into Ted's Tools, following up a lead on another mystery we worked on — and solved — not too long ago. It had sounded like a neat place, the kind of old-fashioned hardware store that carries everything you can imagine.

The sun was warm, and my mind drifted as I sat on the bench. I thought about all the clues we had written down in our mystery notebook, and how none of them added up to much. I thought back over the events of the past week, and shuddered when I remembered that moment when, standing in the middle of a small clearing with a brick in my hand, I'd heard the word, "Freeze!"

"Ugh," I said out loud. Logan and Mal looked at me.

"What?" asked Logan.

"I was just thinking of how awful it was when Officer Cleary was shining that light on me," I explained. "I just stood there, holding that brick, and I couldn't think of a thing to say."

Logan reached out and patted my shoulder, and Mal gave me a sympathetic smile. I looked down at my hands, almost expecting to see a brick in them. A green-painted brick. "Hey!" I said suddenly. "I wonder why the vandals were using a brick with green paint on it. It's not the kind of thing you find just lying around." I looked up again and saw the Ted's Tools sign, and something clicked in my brain. I stood up and headed for the store. Logan and Mal followed me, as if they knew exactly what I was thinking without my having to tell them. When we stepped into the store, a little bell rang and a salesman approached us.

"Can I help you?" asked the man, who wore a name tag that said "Ted."

"I was just wondering," I said, not even bothering to figure out a cover story, "if you've sold any green house paint recently."

"What shade?" he asked. He didn't seem to be curious about why I wanted to know.

I thought for a second, picturing the brick. "Forest," I said firmly. "Forest green."

Fortunately for us, Ted seemed to have a brain like a computer when it came to local home improvement projects. He scratched his head. "Why, I haven't sold much of that at all recently. In fact, I think the last batch of forest green I sold was to — to the Robbins family, for that extension they're building."

I thanked him and we headed out. I wasn't sure if we'd learned anything meaningful, but our stakeout was over. It was time for our BSC meeting.

When we arrived, everyone else was already there, poring over the Stoneybrook Day School yearbook that Shannon had brought. Shannon hadn't been able to think of an Allie in her grade, so she was leafing through the pages, looking for one in the upper grades.

Suddenly, she stopped and pointed to a picture. "Now I know who she is," she said. "Allie Newbern. She's a tenth-grader. I've seen her in the halls lots of times, with her boyfriend."

"Boyfriend?" asked Abby. "That must be the B.R. I saw scribbled all over that notebook of hers that I found at the Martinezes'. Do you know his name?"

"B.R.!" I exclaimed, excited all of a sudden. "This may sound weird — but what if the R stands for Robbins?" Since I'd just heard that

117

name over at Ted's Tools, it was on my mind.

Shannon flipped the pages, looking for the name Robbins. Sure enough, three pages later we found a picture of a boy named Beau Robbins. Shannon shrieked, "That's him! That's her boyfriend!"

"And check out his address," said Kristy, who had grabbed a Stoneybrook phone book and flipped it open to the Rs. I read it, and realized that the Robbins family lived right around the corner from the Martinezes.

"Whoa," I said softly. "I'm starting to see some connections here."

"We'll have to head over there right after school tomorrow," said Kristy. "If we're lucky, maybe things will come together for us. We don't have much time before that meeting, though."

Stacey agreed. "And it doesn't look as if we have any other leads, either," she added. "Jessi and I couldn't find out anything else about Samuel Wolf. We hit a total dead end."

After school the next day, Kristy came home with me. Shannon's mom drove her over, and then the three of us walked over to the Martinezes' neighborhood. We passed their street and kept walking, right up to a green house — a forest green house with what looked like a brand-new brick addition.

As we came closer, I spotted an older — maybe high-school age — boy and a girl in the yard. There was something familiar about the boy, but I didn't figure it out until we had passed the house. (We were pretending to take a casual stroll.)

"That's him!" I hissed to Kristy. "I didn't recognize him from the yearbook picture, but now I see it. He's the one I saw in the woods with Fowler!"

Kristy nodded, excited. "And did you see what they were doing?" she hissed back. "She was smoking. And he was rolling a cigarette. They might be the ones who dropped that empty pack of tobacco!"

"Let's take another look," whispered Shannon. "Just to be sure." We strolled back the other way, and suddenly our cover was blown. Allie had spotted Shannon.

"Hi!" she called. "Don't you go to Stoneybrook Day?"

"Uh, yes," answered Shannon nervously.

"What's up? What are you doing in this neighborhood?" asked Allie. She seemed friendly. Beau just lounged on the grass, smoking and ignoring us.

"I — um, I baby-sit for one of your neighbors," replied Shannon.

Allie smiled. "There are some great kids in this neighborhood," she said. "I've done some baby-sitting around here, too."

Suddenly, I remembered the threatening notes and phone calls Luke had been receiving. All the clues, I realized suddenly, pointed toward one conclusion, a conclusion I didn't want to reach: Allie, this friendly girl, was connected to all the strange happenings at the Martinezes'. And that included the threats to Luke. How could Allie call herself a baby-sitter if she did things like that? Without even thinking about it, I stepped forward. "How could you!" I cried.

"How could I what?" asked Allie, looking confused.

"How could you threaten a little kid like Luke? How could you start a fire in somebody's house, or try to flood somebody's basement?" I was so angry I barely knew what I was saying. "How could you vandalize a neat old place like the mill?"

Kristy was staring at me in disbelief. So was Shannon. Allie just looked surprised and confused.

Beau, however, looked guilty.

"What are you talking about?" Allie asked.

I slowed myself down enough to introduce myself and the others, and to explain what I was talking about and list the clues we'd put together. Allie looked shocked. Finally, she turned to Beau — and he turned away.

"Beau," said Allie quietly. "Beau, what have you done?"

CHAPTER 13

Beau kept his face turned away from Allie. She touched him on the shoulder, but he shrugged off her hand. "Beau?" she asked, in a small voice.

She turned back to face us. "I'm sure there's been some kind of mistake," she said, almost as if she were trying to convince herself.

I could see how upset she was, and suddenly I stopped being so mad. It was hard to stay angry at someone who looked as if she were about to cry. "I wish it *was* a mistake," I said, trying to keep my voice gentle, "but I don't think it is. I think you both know something about that fire."

At that point, Allie stopped looking as if she were going to cry. Instead, she did cry. She didn't sob out loud or anything, but the tears started to roll down her face. "You're right," she said softly. "We do know about the fire. And I'll explain what happened. But really, all that other stuff — I don't know what you're talking about. I didn't flood anybody's basement, or vandalize the mill. And I would never threaten Luke. Never."

I believed her. "But then who — " I began.

Beau interrupted me. "I did it," he said suddenly, in a harsh voice. "I did all those things." He turned to Allie. "Oh, Allie, I'm so sorry. I never meant for you to be involved." He reached out for her, but she stepped back and just looked at him. Her face was white and her lips were pressed together in a straight line.

"Why, Beau?" she asked. "Why?"

He gave a huge sigh. "It's so complicated," he said, shaking his head. "It just grew and grew, and soon I was all tangled up in it. Now there's no way out." He had this sad, trapped look on his face.

Kristy stepped forward. "Okay," she said. "Time out." She made a "T" with her hands. "Obviously, you both have a lot of explaining to do. How about if we start from the beginning?"

Good old Kristy, taking control. Allie and Beau almost looked relieved. "Fine with me," said Beau. His voice sounded more normal now.

"Is there somewhere we can sit down?" asked Shannon.

"Sure. Let's go around back to the patio," said Beau. He led us around the house to a pretty terrace. There was white wicker furniture with green cushions that matched the color of the house. We all sat down. Beau and Allie sat together on a love seat, but I noticed that Allie sat as far from him as she could. I saw her sneaking glances at him, though. She was looking at him as if she didn't recognize him.

We were all quiet for a few moments. Then Beau and Allie both started to talk at the same time.

"We didn't mean — " she began.

"It was an accident — " he said.

Beau waved a hand at Allie. "You start," he said.

She looked at him. "All right," she said. She turned back to us. 'See, the thing is that Beau was over visiting me when I was sitting for Luke and Amalia that day — the day of the fire."

"And the Martinezes didn't know?" I asked.

She shook her head. "They'd asked me not to have anyone over," she admitted. "And I didn't mean to break the rules. He just stopped by for a minute that day, because there was something he wanted to tell me."

I nodded. So far, I could totally relate to the story. I once went through a terrible time after a client of ours discovered that Logan had been coming by when I baby-sat. I had a good reason for having him there (it was because the boy I was sitting for was missing his dad, and Logan seemed to help fill the gap) but still, I didn't ask first. The client was angry — rightfully so — and I was in trouble with her, with the BSC, and especially with Kristy. Kristy insists on the rules being followed at all times. I glanced over at her and I could tell that she didn't have much sympathy for Allie.

Sure enough, Kristy spoke up. "You should have told him to leave," she said.

Allie nodded, looking miserable. "I know," she said. "But instead I asked him to wait a minute, since I was in the middle of a game with Amalia." She paused. "I miss Amalia," she said softly. "She gives the best hugs in the world."

I had a feeling that Allie was a pretty good baby-sitter, even if she *had* broken the rules.

"So then what happened?" asked Shannon.

Beau spoke up. "It was drizzling out, so instead of waiting in the backyard I was waiting in the garage," he said. "Luke saw me, but Allie and I made him promise not to tell his parents that I'd been there."

I nodded. Poor Luke. He'd been keeping that secret for a long time.

"I was smoking," Beau continued. "And

when I finished, I tossed my cigarette butt away. It was out. Or at least I thought it was."

"That's when I finished up with Amalia," said Allie. "I let Beau into the kitchen, just for a few minutes."

"And the next thing we knew, we smelled smoke," finished Beau. "I guess my cigarette had landed in some bags of newspaper that were waiting to be recycled."

Allie shut her eyes and frowned, as if she were remembering something painful. "I told Luke to take Amalia outside," she said. "That was my first concern: making sure the kids were safe. Then Beau and I went into the garage and tried to put out the fire. I know now that I should have left the house, too, and called nine-one-one. But I was so afraid of having the Martinezes find out what happened that I wasn't thinking straight at the time. We used the fire extinguisher, but the fire was too far along and the fire extinguisher was half empty to start with." She was speaking quickly. "It was horrible," she said.

"We did everything we could," said Beau. "Finally, just as the fire was almost under control, I heard sirens. They were off in the distance, but I knew they were coming our way fast, and I knew the firefighters would take care of everything. I opened the garage door so they could move right in on the fire."

"That's when I told him to run," said Allie. "It was bad enough to have to tell the Martinezes about the fire. I didn't want them to know Beau had been the one who started it. I didn't even want them to know he had been there." She leaned back in her seat and sighed. "That's it," she said. "That's everything I know about it. I told the Martinezes that I didn't know how the fire started, and then I felt so bad about lying to them that I couldn't even stand to be around them. So I said I had to quit. I felt terrible about that, leaving them in the lurch."

"Whew!" I said. "That's quite a story." I could see that Allie felt better already. Telling the truth can have that effect.

"But it's not the whole story," Kristy reminded us. "What about those threatening notes and calls to Luke?"

Beau put his face in his hands. "That was me," he admitted.

Allie glared at him. "How could you, Beau?" she asked. "How could you do that to Luke?"

"I know it was wrong," said Beau. "I see that now. But when I was in the middle of it, I was just so scared."

"Scared of what?" asked Shannon.

"Scared that the Martinezes would find out, I guess," said Beau carefully. He sounded as if he were still hiding something. He stood up. "Hey, would anyone like a Coke? I'm dying of thirst." Before we could stop him, he loped off into the house.

Allie looked at us, and then down at her hands. "I can't believe he did that," she said. "Poor Luke. He's just a little kid."

"He wouldn't have told, either," I said. "Luke seems to be pretty good at keeping secrets. Nobody had to threaten him."

"I'm going to go over and talk to him," said Allie. "I want to apologize, and try to explain."

"Good," said Kristy. "Maybe if you do, he'll start to trust baby-sitters again."

Just then, Beau came back outside carrying a six-pack of soda. He handed the cans around, popped one for himself, and sat next to Allie again. She wouldn't look at him.

"Beau," I said. "There's more to this story. What about the night of the vandalism at Ambrose's Sawmill? I saw you in the woods that night. I know I did."

Beau bit his lip. "It's all connected," he explained. "See, Fowler saw me running away from the fire that day, and I guess he put two and two together. He blackmailed me, basically. He said that if I didn't help him out with a few 'errands,' he'd tell the police on me. Fowler had no idea that Luke knew about me starting the fire, but I told Luke he did. Luke and his friend Steig were scared of Fowler after that, and that helped keep Luke quiet."

"Oh, Beau!" cried Allie.

"What did he want you to do?" I asked.

"I was supposed to mess up the sawmill," said Beau, "which is what I was doing that night. And I was supposed to flood that basement."

"Hold on a second," said Kristy. "Are you sure it was Reginald Fowler asking you to do these things, and not his twin?" She turned to me and Shannon. "I mean, why would Fowler want to vandalize the mill? If his twin brother wanted to sabotage the deal, that would make more sense. Right?"

I shrugged. I was totally confused. "I guess," I said. "Or maybe he was trying to frame his brother, or maybe he was trying to help his brother by framing *us*, which would help quiet the opposition to the project." I was starting to have a headache. "Anyway, the guy Beau was dealing with *must* have been the twin, since Fowler was in California both times."

"I bet the twins are enemies," said Shannon. "Samuel seems to be working behind Reginald's back, doing these things when he's out of town. I bet they haven't seen each other in years. Reginald probably doesn't know that Samuel is in the area."

"I didn't even know Fowler had a twin,"

said Beau. "All I know is that the guy I was involved with introduced himself to me as Mr. Fowler. And he has one more job for me. I'm supposed to do it tonight, before that town council meeting takes place."

"What's the job?" asked Shannon.

"I don't know," said Beau. "I'm supposed to be at this cabin on the edge of Miller's Park at six, and he'll tell me then. The meeting is at seven."

"The cabin!" I exclaimed. "That must be the cabin where they lived when they were little."

There was silence for a second as we all digested this. Now that we knew the whole story — or most of it, anyway — what were we going to do about it?

"Well, we're going to be at that cabin, too," Kristy declared suddenly. She had this gleam in her eyes, and I knew she was coming up with a plan. I could practically see the wheels turning inside her brain. "And we'll make sure Reginald comes, too. It's time for the twins to meet up again."

"How will we make him come?" I asked.

"We'll tell him we've set up a special meeting and we'll act as if we're ready to make a deal with him. Like that we'll shut up about the project if he gives us some money or something. He'll go along with it."

"What if he doesn't?" Shannon asked.

130

"We'll have Sergeant Johnson in the background," said Kristy. She'd thought of everything. "He'll be our backup."

We had a plan. I wasn't sure it was a great plan, but it was a plan.

CHAPTER 14

We left Allie and Beau sitting together on the wicker love seat, talking quietly. It looked as if they were going to make up.

Kristy and Shannon headed off to talk to Sergeant Johnson and make arrangements for that evening's meeting at the cabin.

I, meanwhile, had some other business to take care of. I headed down the block to the Martinezes', knowing that I needed to talk to Luke.

He was playing outside when I arrived at the house. "Hey, Luke," I called. He looked up and gave me a little wave, but he didn't smile. I noticed that his parents' car was in the driveway, so I figured they must be home from work. I took a deep breath and decided it was best to talk to everyone at once.

"Where's Amalia?" I asked as I approached Luke.

"At a friend's house," Luke answered, without looking up at me.

"Luke, I need to talk to you and your parents. Can we go inside?"

Luke shrugged and nodded. I could tell he wasn't thrilled about the idea.

And he was even less thrilled when he and I and his parents sat down around the kitchen table and I launched right into the story. I told them everything I knew, everything I'd just learned from Beau and Allie. I watched Mr. and Mrs. Martinez's faces as I talked, and saw them go from shock to anger to understanding. Mr. Martinez kept an arm around Luke's shoulders.

"So that's the whole story," I finished finally. I looked at Luke. "Luke, do you understand what this means? You don't have to be a silent witness anymore. You don't have to be afraid of Beau, or Fowler, or anyone."

Luke nodded. I saw a single tear working its way down his cheek. I felt a jolt of sympathy for him. Poor kid. It must have been such stress to keep Beau's secret. And he must have been so frightened by the threats.

"Luke, it's okay now," Mr. Martinez assured him. "It's over."

Mrs. Martinez sighed. "I suppose we could press charges against the Robbins boy, but I think it's better just to let things go back to normal. After all, he was wrong to threaten Luke, but he was being intimidated himself."

"He should have gone to the police," I said.

"Of course he should have," said Mr. Martinez. "But I think he was simply too scared."

"Like me," said Luke. "I was too scared to tell you. But I guess I should have. It's not always a good thing to keep a secret."

Suddenly, I remembered that Luke might have one more secret. "Luke," I said. "Is there something else you need to tell us? Something about what's hidden under your bed?" Maybe Cary hadn't been kidding about that.

Luke jumped up from the table. "Oh, right!" he said. "Wait here!" He ran out of the kitchen and up the stairs.

Mr. and Mrs. Martinez glanced at each other and laughed. "It's good to see him happy again," Mrs. Martinez remarked. "He's been so mopey, and I had no idea why. I hope he can put this all behind him now."

Just then, Luke ran back into the kitchen, clutching a rolled-up piece of paper. "Steig and I found this in the mill one day." He spread it out on the table. We all bent forward to see what it was.

"Whoa!" I breathed.

"My lord!" said Mrs. Martinez.

"I don't believe it." Mr. Martinez gave a long, low whistle.

"I wasn't sure what to do with it," continued Luke. "I thought if anybody caught me with it, they might blame me for making that mess at the mill. But I didn't want to throw it away, because I knew it was important." He looked a little bit proud, and a little bit nervous.

"It's *very* important," I said, still staring at it. "It" was a hand-drawn map of Stoneybrook, signed by "R. Fowler." At the top right-hand corner, it said, "Long-Term Town Plan."

The map was shocking. Fowler's vision for Stoneybrook included a huge industrial complex that wiped out most of the town. Massive apartment buildings would be built to replace the houses he'd have to tear down. And instead of downtown stores, he envisioned three gigantic malls on the outskirts of town. To serve all the increased traffic, there would be new highways running everywhere. Including, I noticed, one that went right through my backyard.

"He must be kidding!" I said.

"I don't think he is," said Mrs. Martinez slowly. "I think he's dead serious."

"And he has the money and the influence to pull it off, too," added Mr. Martinez. "He'll start small — like, with this Miller's Park project. The town won't even realize what he's up to until it's too late."

"Oh, yes they will!" declared Mrs. Martinez, taking the map and rolling it up. "They'll realize it tonight, when we bring this map to the town council meeting."

"So it's good that I saved it?" Luke asked.

"It's great," Mr. Martinez told him. "Now, how about if we go outside for a game of catch and forget about all this stuff for a while?"

I stood up. Hearing Mrs. Martinez talk about the meeting reminded me of another meeting I had to attend: the one between Reginald Fowler and his twin brother.

Luke let me give him a quick hug. In fact, he even hugged me back a little bit. Mr. and Mrs. Martinez both shook my hand and thanked me. They said they'd see me at the town council meeting, which was only a little over an hour away.

I headed for the cabin where Beau was supposed to meet Fowler, and arrived there just in time. As I approached the clearing where the old, tumble-down cabin sits, I heard Kristy call my name. "Mary Anne! Over here," she said quietly.

I joined her, Shannon, and Sergeant Johnson in their hiding spot, which was behind a row of trees, but close enough to the cabin so that we'd be able to hear any conversations through its open windows.

"Is he here yet?" I whispered, after I'd said hello to Sergeant Johnson.

"Beau's here," replied Shannon. She checked her watch. "And the man he's supposed to meet is due any minute."

"What about Fowler?" I asked. "I mean Reginald, not the twin."

"He'll be here soon, too," said Kristy. "It wasn't hard to convince him to come; he sounded interested right away."

"Shh!" hissed Shannon. "Here comes the twin now."

We ducked behind the trees and watched as a car drove up. A man who looked exactly like Reginald Fowler climbed out and approached the cabin. Without pausing, he opened the door, and walked inside.

We all stopped breathing for a second and strained to hear what he and Beau would say to each other. The words came through loud and clear.

"Good. You're here."

"Yes, sir." That was Beau's voice.

"Ready to do that job for me?"

"Yes, sir," Beau said again.

"Good. What I want you to do is torch this place."

"The cabin?"

"Right. The cabin. Do it tonight."

"How do I — ?"

"There's a container of gasoline outside in my car." Footsteps. The man was preparing to leave. I gasped. Now what? Fowler was supposed to show up any minute. Our whole plan would be blown if the twin left now.

Beau must have been thinking the same thing. "Uh, sir?" he asked, plainly trying to stall the man.

"What is it?"

"Um — do you have a brother?" Beau sounded desperate.

Silence. The footsteps stopped, as if the man had stopped in his tracks. "A brother? No, no. I don't have — "

Just then, another car pulled up. Reginald Fowler had arrived. Before he could enter the cabin, his twin brother opened the door. The two men stared at each other in silence. They looked exactly alike. I couldn't believe it. And both of them wore identical frowns. They did not seem at all happy to see each other.

My heart was pounding hard. Could they hear it?

Finally, Fowler spoke. "Samuel. I should have known you were in town. Who else would try to sabotage all my plans?"

"I just didn't want you to destroy this town, John," said the twin.

"It's Reginald now," said Fowler. "Reginald Fowler. John Wolfer no longer exists."

"I see," said Samuel. "I changed my name, too. More than once. Trying to escape the past, I suppose. These days I call myself Samuel Wolf."

"Well, Samuel Wolf," said Fowler with an unpleasant smile. "What's it to you if I destroy this town? What has it ever done for us? I'll be happy when it's destroyed, along with all the memories."

Samuel shook his head. "You have it all wrong," he said. "It's not the town's fault our mother died. And ruining the town isn't going to bring her back to life. Somehow your mind has become twisted over the years."

"And yours hasn't?" snapped Fowler. "You, who sneak around like a petty vandal, trying to set me up for failure?"

Samuel hung his head. "I suppose there might have been better ways of going about it," he said. "But I was desperate. I just wanted to stop you, and I knew you wouldn't listen to reason. After all, I am your twin. I know you better than anyone does. And anyway, I never did the actual vandalism. I hired somebody else for the dirty work."

Just then Sergeant Johnson stepped out from our hiding place. "Thank you for your full confession," he said, flashing his badge as he handcuffed Samuel. Reginald looked as if he were about to run off, but three other policemen stepped out of the shadows and he froze.

"You can't arrest me," said Fowler. "I haven't done anything illegal."

"That may be true," said Sergeant Johnson. "But I think the people of Stoneybrook have a right to hear what your plans are for their town. Why don't you come along with me and tell them?"

Fowler frowned, but didn't resist as Sergeant Johnson walked him out of the clearing.

We watched them go, and then stepped out of our hiding spot to follow them. Meanwhile, the other police officers were reading Samuel Wolfer and Beau (whom they'd gone into the cabin to find) their rights. As we passed them, I realized that one of the policemen was Officer Cleary, and I smiled at him.

He nodded at me. "We'll bring these two down to the station," he said. "But then I think I'll join you at the meeting. It's going to be an interesting evening down at Town Hall."

CHAPTER 15

The meeting room was packed. By the time we arrived, every seat had been taken and lots of people were standing along the back wall. We squeezed in, finding places to stand. There was a buzz in the air, a tense feeling. Seven men and women — the town council members — sat at a long, horseshoe-shaped desk in the front of the room, facing the audience. There was a man setting up a video camera on a tripod. The town council meetings are broadcast live on the local public access channel.

I spotted Mr. and Mrs. Martinez and Luke (they must have found a sitter for Amalia) in the third row of seats, and I waved. All three of them grinned and waved back.

Reginald Fowler sat near the back, next to a glowering Sergeant Johnson. Fowler looked trapped — and angry.

Suddenly I heard a loud knocking noise, and I turned to the front and saw that one of the council members was banging a gavel on the desk. The crowd fell silent.

The gray-haired woman who had banged the gavel stood up. "Welcome to tonight's meeting," she said in a friendly voice. "We realize we have a controversial subject to deal with this evening, and we'd like to ask for your cooperation. Let's keep our emotions under control. Remember, we welcome all public input, but you may only speak when the chair — that's me! — recognizes you." She smiled around at everyone. Then she sat down and opened the meeting.

What happened after that was pretty much a big blur. First there was some boring stuff; lawyers presenting proposals, other lawyers presenting counter-proposals, things like that. The big question was whether Miller's Park should be "zoned for phase three development" or, instead, be named an official historic landmark. Then the chair recognized Fowler, and he gave this whole totally phony speech about how he only had the best interests of Stoneybrook at heart. Kristy was shaking her head and looking furious, and I had to hold her back so she wouldn't start a scene.

After Fowler spoke, a whole lot of other people raised their hands and spoke. Some talked about how they supported Fowler, and thought the development of Miller's Park would be good for Stoneybrook. Others spoke about why they opposed the idea. The best speaker was a man from the Historical Society, who talked about why it was important to preserve places like the old sawmill.

I'd noticed Luke's hand sticking up for quite a while before he was recognized. I knew he and his parents had brought the map that showed Fowler's horrible plan, and I knew that it was an important piece of evidence. I was worried that the chairwoman wouldn't see Luke, but finally she did. "Yes?" she asked. "The boy in front, here."

Luke stood up. "I brought something I found at Ambrose's Sawmill," he said, in a voice that was only slightly shaky. I was proud of him. "It's a map," he continued. "A map and a plan. Of what Mr. Fowler *really* wants to do to our town."

"Why don't you bring it up here?" asked the chairwoman.

Luke squeezed his way down the row of seats, walked up to the front, and handed the rolled-up map to her.

"Thank you," she said. She unrolled the map, gazed at it briefly, and frowned. Then she passed it along to the other council members, and turned to face Reginald Fowler. "Mr. Fowler, what can you tell me about this document?" she asked.

Fowler's face was white. "It's not — it's just a preliminary — that's my private property, and it was stolen!" By the time he finished, he was yelling and his face had turned from white to red. Sergeant Johnson put a hand on his shoulder, as if to calm him down. Fowler shrugged it off. Then he stood up, shoved his way out of the row of seats, and stomped out of the room.

That was the most dramatic point of the evening. After that, it quieted down a lot. The council members discussed the map, listened to more testimony from the audience, and finally, after about an hour and a half, the chairwoman declared the public part of the meeting over.

"I think we have all the information we need to make our decision," she said. "Thank you for coming. Our decision will appear in tomorrow's paper."

Guess what? We won. It's true! It was the lead story in the paper. The council decided to turn down Fowler's proposal. And that's not all. They also decided to designate Miller's Park and Ambrose's Sawmill official historic landmarks, which means nobody can ever develop or change them.

At our BSC meeting the next day, we toasted the decision with punch that Claud had made by combining ginger ale with raspberry-apple juice. She'd also laid out a huge spread of junk food: Twinkies, Ring-Dings, Ranch-Style Doritos, Chee•tos, and Smartfood, just for starters. (She'd put aside some Snickers bars for "dessert.") She'd also provided pretzels and fruit, for Stacey and anyone else who wanted it.

"Here's to Miller's Park!" said Stacey, holding up her cup. We all "clinked" our cups.

"Here's to Luke," I added, and we clinked again.

"Here's to the BSC detective team!" said Claudia. Another round of clinking.

"And here's to Reginald Fowler," said Kristy.

We all stared at her. "What?" I asked. "Are you out of your mind?"

She shrugged. "Well, he's the one who made all this excitement possible."

We cracked up, and clinked one more time.

Just then, Claudia's sister Janine poked her head into the room. "Congratulations," she said. "I thought you might want to see this." She held out a white envelope, and Kristy stood up to take it.

"It's from the mayor's office!" exclaimed Kristy, after she'd examined the envelope. "Hand-delivered, too. There's no stamp."

"Open it!" said Abby. "What are you waiting for?"

Kristy tore the envelope open and shook out a letter. She unfolded it and began to read. "It's from the head of the Stoneybrook park system," she said. "It says, 'Dear Members of the Baby-sitters Club. In honor of your help in preserving Miller's Park for posterity, we'd like to notify you that the area surrounding Ambrose's Sawmill will be renamed Baby-sitters Walk.' "

"Cool!" said Jessi.

"Awesome," said Abby. "We'll be part of an official historical landmark."

"Excellent publicity," said Kristy.

"Wow!" I said. "That's so nice of them."

"Interesting," commented Janine, who was still standing in the doorway. "Very interesting."

"What do you mean, *interesting*?" asked Claud. "Don't you think it's great?"

"Actually, I find it rather peculiar," said Janine.

"Peculiar? Why?" asked Stacey.

"Because Stoneybrook doesn't *have* a park system," said Janine.

"It must!" I said. I grabbed the phone book from Claudia's bed table and checked the "Town of Stoneybrook" listings. Janine was right. There was no park system. "Is this some kind of joke?" I asked.

"Let me see that letter," said Claudia. Kristy

handed it over, and Claudia examined it. "Look at this signature," she said. "A.F. Nilter. What kind of name is that?"

I looked over her shoulder. Then I gasped. "Read it backwards!" I said. "Nilter equals Retlin! This is Cary's work. He must be out for revenge, because I accused him of being involved in the fire."

"But what does the A.F. stand for?" asked Mal.

"I think I know," said Abby, with a little smile. "April Fool!"

"Oh, ha-ha," said Kristy. "We've been tricked once too often by Cary Retlin. This is the last straw. No way are we going to let him have the last word. This means war!"

Ann M. Martin

About the Author

ANN MATTHEWS MARTIN was born on August 12, 1955. She grew up in Princeton, NJ, with her parents and her younger sister, Jane.

Although Ann used to be a teacher and then an editor of children's books, she's now a full-time writer. She gets the ideas for her books from many different places. Some are based on personal experiences. Others are based on childhood memories and feelings. Many are written about contemporary problems or events.

All of Ann's characters, even the members of the Baby-sitters Club, are made up. (So is Stoneybrook.) But many of her characters are based on real people. Sometimes Ann names her characters after people she knows, other times she chooses names she likes.

In addition to the Baby-sitters Club books, Ann Martin has written many other books for children. Her favorite is *Ten Kids, No Pets* because she loves big families and she loves animals. Her favorite Baby-sitters Club book is *Kristy's Big Day*. (By the way, Kristy is her favorite baby-sitter!)

Ann M. Martin now lives in New York with her cats, Gussie and Woody. Her hobbies are reading, sewing, and needlework — especially making clothes for children.

Look for #25

KRISTY AND THE
MIDDLE SCHOOL VANDAL

Someone screamed. Something crashed.

We all jumped.

"Behind the curtain," said Mary Anne, pointing.

Words like "sabotage" and "Cary" and "uh-oh" went through my head. But before I could act, the door next to the stage opened, and Mr. Kingbridge walked in with a group of adults, among them Mr. Oates and a woman who was holding a microcassette recorder.

"I'm glad that the *News* is taking an interest in this problem, Ms. Burnstein," Mr. Oates said in a clear, carrying voice.

Ms. Burnstein just nodded.

Another crash, another scream.

Mr. Kingbridge jumped up onto the stage without hesitation and yanked the curtain aside.

We all gasped at the chaos that met our eyes.

All the scenery from the last school play,

which had been propped against the back wall, had been torn apart, some of it shredded. And the props — furniture, rugs, a bicycle, and a ladder — had all been tied together in the center of the stage with the ropes used to move the backstage props around. The knots looked numerous, and huge. Someone would probably need a saw to cut through the heavy rope.

We hurried forward. And stopped.

Clearly visible in the middle of the stage floorboards, in front of the tied-up furniture, were the letters "MK" in green chalk — although a different shade from the green I'd seen on the bathroom door.

"What's the meaning of this?" demanded Mr. Kingbridge in an angry voice.

"Out of control! See!" said Mr. Oates to the *Stoneybrook News* reporter. She was raising a camera to take pictures.

Read all the books
about **Mary Anne**
in the Baby-sitters Club series
by Ann M. Martin

#60 *Mary Anne's Makeover*
Everyone loves the new Mary Anne — *except* the BSC!

#66 *Maid Mary Anne*
Mary Anne's a baby-sitter — not a housekeeper!

#73 *Mary Anne and Miss Priss*
What will Mary Anne do with a kid who is *too* perfect?

#79 *Mary Anne Breaks the Rules*
Boyfriends and baby-sitting don't always mix.

#86 *Mary Anne and Camp BSC*
Mary Anne is in for loads of summer fun!

#93 *Mary Anne and the Memory Garden*
Mary Anne must say a sad good-bye to a friend.

Mysteries:

 # 5 *Mary Anne and the Secret in the Attic*
Mary Anne discovers a secret about her past and now she's afraid of the future!

#13 *Mary Anne and the Library Mystery*
There's a readathon going on and someone's setting fires in the Stoneybrook Library!

#20 *Mary Anne and the Zoo Mystery*
Someone is freeing the animals at the Bedford Zoo!

#24 *Mary Anne and the Silent Witness*
Luke knows who did it — but can Mary Anne convince him to tell?

Portrait Collection:

Mary Anne's Book
Mary Anne's own life story.

THE BABY-SITTERS CLUB®

by Ann M. Martin

Collect and read these exciting BSC Super Specials, Mysteries, and Super Mysteries along with your favorite Baby-sitters Club books!

BSC Super Specials

❑ BBK44240-6	Baby-sitters on Board! Super Special #1	$3.95
❑ BBK44239-2	Baby-sitters' Summer Vacation Super Special #2	$3.95
❑ BBK43973-1	Baby-sitters' Winter Vacation Super Special #3	$3.95
❑ BBK42493-9	Baby-sitters' Island Adventure Super Special #4	$3.95
❑ BBK43575-2	California Girls! Super Special #5	$3.95
❑ BBK43576-0	New York, New York! Super Special #6	$3.95
❑ BBK44963-X	Snowbound! Super Special #7	$3.95
❑ BBK44962-X	Baby-sitters at Shadow Lake Super Special #8	$3.95
❑ BBK45661-X	Starring The Baby-sitters Club! Super Special #9	$3.95
❑ BBK45674-1	Sea City, Here We Come! Super Special #10	$3.95
❑ BBK47015-9	The Baby-sitters Remember Super Special #11	$3.95
❑ BBK48308-0	Here Come the Bridesmaids! Super Special #12	$3.95

BSC Mysteries

❑ BAI44084-5	#1	Stacey and the Missing Ring	$3.50
❑ BAI44085-3	#2	Beware Dawn!	$3.50
❑ BAI44799-8	#3	Mallory and the Ghost Cat	$3.50
❑ BAI44800-5	#4	Kristy and the Missing Child	$3.50
❑ BAI44801-3	#5	Mary Anne and the Secret in the Attic	$3.50
❑ BAI44961-3	#6	The Mystery at Claudia's House	$3.50
❑ BAI44960-5	#7	Dawn and the Disappearing Dogs	$3.50
❑ BAI44959-1	#8	Jessi and the Jewel Thieves	$3.50
❑ BAI44958-3	#9	Kristy and the Haunted Mansion	$3.50

More titles ➡

The Baby-sitters Club books continued...